A Naughty List for Christmas

Sugar Peak Resort

Kat Summers

This book is a work of fiction from the author's imagination. Though inspired by the world around us, all of the characters, places, and events are fictional and not based on any one source. Any resemblance is entirely coincidental.

A Naughty List for Christmas

Proofed by Editing by Bobbi

Cover by MR Creations

ISBN-13: 979-8-9897343-3-7

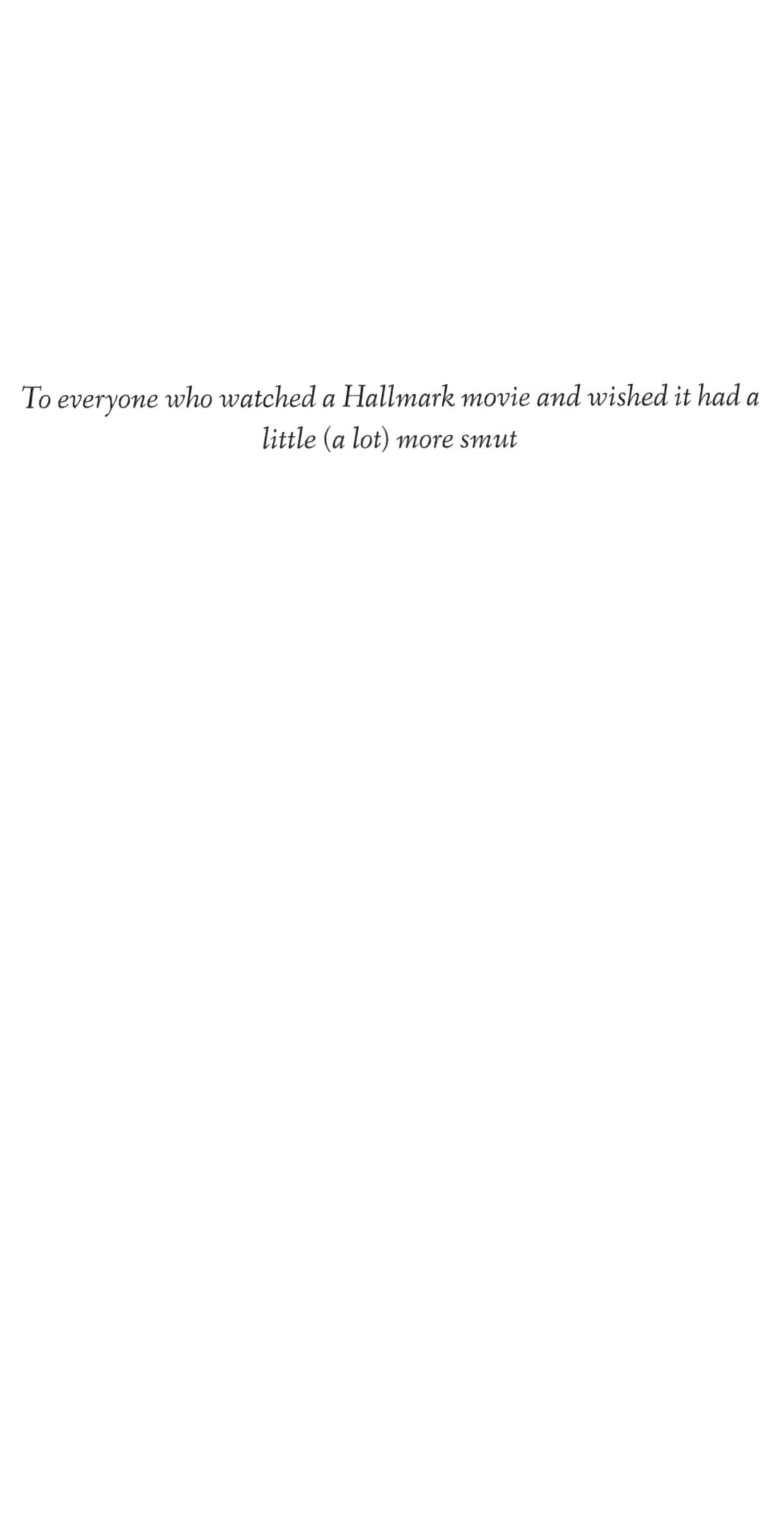

To everyone who watched a Hallmark movie and wished it had a little (a lot) more smut

Dicktionary/Author's Note

Though a short read, I hope this story gives you all the holiday goodness you hope for. *A Naughty List for Christmas* is very high on the spice scale an it is an integral part of the plot. That said, you can avoid the explicitness or go right to it, in chapters 11, 14, 15, 17, 18, and 22.

1

Mia

"You know, if we slipped something other than sage into the stuffing, we could really make this Thanksgiving something special," my sister-in-law, Rory, whispers conspiratorially.

"We're not drugging the stuffing," I chastise. "Besides, Nonna would notice."

"Fine. What about the pumpkin pie? Hardly anyone eats it anyway."

"You'd have better luck with the pecan pie, I think, but still no."

"You're no fun," she pouts.

"Is that why you're spending your time here with me instead of out there with everyone else? You know you, as a Ricci by marriage, don't have to help in the kitchen. You're free to join the men in the living room."

At that moment loud groans can be heard from the room in question. The Giants must have made a bad play.

Despite my family immigrating to North Dakota in the '80s, we are still diehard Giants fans for some reason. Naturally, all the Ricci men have to watch their team play and can't be bothered with silly things like preparing a twenty-person feast, as if they've ever helped to begin with.

"Technically, I still go by Bennet—much to your parents' disdain—but I would much rather talk to you than the Neanderthals in there. I don't think Tony is ready to mediate a fight between me and your Uncle Mario again," Rory retorts. "Isn't Steven a Vikings fan? What's his excuse for not helping?"

I blush at the mention of my boyfriend. Because she's not wrong. Steven practically bleeds purple and gold. But he wouldn't be caught dead helping in the kitchen while all the other men weren't. In fact, I can't remember the last time he cooked something not on the grill.

"He didn't want to be excluded," I mumble. Rory shoots me a knowing glance. She's made her feelings on Steven well known since day one. I can't say she's wrong, but we aren't all as lucky as she is.

Rory and my brother Tony met in college. He may have been the upperclassman, but she didn't give him the time of day. It took an entire semester for him to get her number. Once she gave him a chance, though, they were inseparable. They've been together through med school, residency, and Rory starting her women's apparel empire. They took the leap and got married five years ago and have been couple goals ever since.

Steven and I are pretty much the opposite. He was friends with my brother all through high school. Being several years younger, he didn't give me a second glance until he came home after getting his teaching degree. With no other friends in town, we started hanging out and eventually dating.

Despite being together only a couple years less than Rory and Tony, we haven't gotten past the living together stage. My mother has almost given up asking me when we'll get married. Almost. There are only so many ways I can say, "Whenever he asks," before people get the hint that I'm wondering, too.

Truthfully, I'm not sure what we're waiting on. First it was for me to graduate, then it was to get stable jobs. Last time I asked, Steven wanted to own our own home, which is not exactly an easy feat on a teacher and program coordinator salary. I pick up side party planning gigs here and there to help save up, but it never seems to be enough.

We've been renting a house from his aunt for the last six years. Every time something good comes up for sale, Steven drags his feet and we miss out. With a population of only 6,000, homes don't come up very often. I've floated around the idea of moving somewhere else, maybe joining my brother in Minneapolis or even Fargo, but he wants to stay near his mom.

"How are things with you and Steven?" my sister-in-law asks.

As she watches me expectantly, I have no idea how to explain to girl-power-icon Aurora-fucking-Bennet that Steven is fine. Our relationship is fine. Everything is just fine. He hasn't made me come in seven months, but everything is fine and dandy.

As if to squash any sexual thought, my brother chooses that moment to walk in.

"There's half of my favorite women," he coos, giving us both a kiss on the top of the head. "Need any help?"

"Careful, honey. You'll ruin the streak of Ricci men being absolutely useless in the kitchen if you keep it up," his wife quips.

"Rory, darling. Light of my life. We both know if I let our contribution come from you, everyone would go home ill."

"I guess it's a good thing you're a doctor, then," she sasses back. But he's not wrong. Icon she is, she can't cook for shit.

"She was trying to poison the stuffing," I pipe in, laughing when Tony freezes mid-reach for a crouton.

"Drug. Not poison," she defends. "I thought it would help everyone mellow out, so they'll stop asking us when we're going to have kids and Mia when she's getting engaged. You'd think they'd have new material by now."

"I don't think Mom will ever give that line of questioning up," I sigh. Rory pats my hand empathetically while Tony offers a sad smile.

"You want me to talk to him? He's been dragging my baby sister on long enough."

"I don't want to mess up y'all's friendship."

Rory scoffs. "The only reason he's still in the group is because he's with you. The rest of the guys outgrew him years ago."

As true as it may be, Steven would never see it that way. Ten years in and he sometimes manages to still make me feel like the interloper; as if he's doing me a favor by dating me. My parents certainly seem to think he's a catch. They only protested a little when I told them we'd be "living in sin" before getting married. Though, I think they assumed marriage was an eventuality. At this point, I'm not sure.

"If you really want to help me, Tones, we can tell her about the time you snuck out when you were seventeen to make out with Rachel Crouch behind the gas station."

"You wouldn't." He gapes.

I shrug in response. "It's the ace up my sleeve."

2

Mia

THE NEXT WEEK is largely uneventful. Sitting at my desk, I am preparing for the holiday shopping event I host for the residents each year. When I first took this job after getting my event management degree from the local community college, I thought it would be boring. I thought wrong. The residents may be old, but our last bingo tournament had more drama than the soaps they watch.

Most of the residents aren't able-bodied enough to brave the crowds and the cold to purchase holiday gifts, and not tech savvy enough to shop online. Instead, we stock up throughout the year on toys, home decor, and other items they might want to gift their loved ones.

Since most of their money goes to pay for their fees here, everyone gets a set amount of tickets to spend. They can also earn tickets throughout the year by winning different contests, being named "Resident of the Month," and a few other means. I have a sneaking suspicion there is a black market for these tickets, based on how many men I've seen Louise with this year and how many more tickets she has than everyone else, but some things are better left unconfirmed.

Giving my email one final glance before I open the floodgates, I see a new message from a name I don't recognize.

I am sorry if this email catches you off guard. I got your contact information from Aurora Bennet. She is a mentor of mine and when I mentioned that I was seeking an event manager, she told me I had to talk to you.

I work for Engenica Cybersecurity as the assistant to Thiago Oliveira de Santos, CEO. We are opening a new resort in Sugar Peak, BC. Due to unforeseen circumstances, our event manager along with some other staff were unable to continue their duties. Aurora sang your praises and said you might be available to start ASAP.

Would you be able to chat tomorrow to discuss the opportunity? I'm sure you will find the compensation and benefits very competitive. The offer includes room and board at the resort. We are looking for someone who is able to start December 1 as we just recently opened our doors for guests and anticipate a busy holiday season. Aurora already discussed your credentials with me. And frankly, her endorsement is all the reference I need.

If you are interested at all, let's hop on the phone.
Thank you for your time,
Hadley Knight

I stare at the email for an inappropriate amount of time. I am in no way qualified to run events at a fancy resort. A really fancy resort, I discover when I visit their website. I plan movie nights for senior citizens, the occasional child's birthday party, and help out with prom. What was Rory thinking?

Still, I can't help but be flattered and intrigued. I allow myself a moment to imagine how it might be to have a job at this beautiful resort. I can already see family nights in the game room and wine tastings in the lounge.

After five minutes of enjoying the fantasy, I close my computer and make my way down the hall to the multi-purpose room. As nice of an offer as it is, it's not one that can ever be a reality for me. Steven would have no interest in moving. And my mother? My mother cried for a month when Tony didn't come home after graduation. No, my life is here, breaking up fights between old men over toys.

"I had it first!" I hear a voice yell as I enter the room. The residents must have sweet-talked the other staff into letting them start early. Heading over to see what the fuss is about, I spot Peter and Rodney both holding on to a portable chess set.

"I saw it first. You used your turbo speed scooter to get over here before me," Rodney argues.

"Fellas, what seems to be the issue?" I ask.

"This smarmy jackass is trying to steal my grandson's Christmas gift!" he replies.

"Don't cuss in front of her. She's a lady," Peter chastises. I shoot him an amused glance. He and I both know the filth that spilled from his month when he lost the annual shuffleboard tournament.

"I've met your grandson. He doesn't have the brains to play a game that doesn't include a candy cane forest or a mustached plumber," he adds.

Holding in my laugh is hard, but I manage. Rodney's grandson, Seth, is a sweet preteen boy, but he isn't a genius by any means—not that I would tell his grandfather that.

"Isn't your grandson a Boy Scout?" I ask. "There is a very cool headlamp over on the outdoors table. It has three different light settings."

"He might like that," Rodney grunts, walking off to check it out.

"Thanks, sweet cheeks," Peter says once he is out of earshot. "His grandson was more likely to swallow the pieces than play with them."

"I don't think that's true." I laugh. "I didn't realize you enjoyed chess."

"I don't. But strip poker is getting old. Gotta mix it up, ya know."

I choke on air, sputtering for a response. Before I can give one, he winks and scooters away to check out the candy selection. Silent generation, my ass.

After mediating a few more quarrels, I let the other staff take over the squabbling and man the library table. Thoroughly picked through, I begin to arrange them into genres for easy browsing.

"If you're looking for any good romance, Louise and Edna picked the pile dry."

"Edna, really?" I ask Doris, my favorite resident. "I didn't think she was the type to enjoy smut."

"She hid them under the new quilt she picked up, but I saw them," she notes conspiratorially.

"I guess I'll have to stick with eBooks, then."

"Oh, child. You shouldn't be reading these books. You should be living them. We use them to remember our glory days, but you should be making out in dugouts and getting felt up on tour buses, not reading about it. Get those orgasms in while you can."

I can't help but blush at this 80-year-old woman telling me to get more orgasms. "I think you've been spending too much time with Louise. And maybe Peter."

"Told you about our strip poker league, did he? That old coot can't keep a secret."

"League?!"

"Don't worry your pretty little head about it." She waves dismissively. "You should be worrying about getting out of here and living a little."

"If I did that, who would make sure you get the best prizes at bingo?" I don't, but we like to pretend I save the best for her.

"Any schmuck could run the bingo cage! No offense, dear."

"Offense taken! Besides, you know my life and my family are here. Steven and I are buying a house soon."

She scoffs. "You've been saying that for two years now. That boy is in no rush. He's getting the milk for free."

Again, offense taken. But I don't verbalize it this time. It's the same thing my mother has been not-so-subtly hinting at since we hit the one year mark of living together with no house. She thinks I should move out and make Steven realize how much he needs me. I'm pretty sure he would just move back in with his mother.

Noting she hit a nerve, Doris takes my hand gently. "Can I give you some advice as an old woman who lived the life everyone expected her to?"

"Of course."

"Run."

"What?"

"You're too bright for a town like this. You deserve to see the world and find someone who wants to give it to you. Don't get me wrong, I loved my Edgar and my kids, but I always wonder what my life would have been like if I'd taken that nursing post in Sioux Falls. It may not have been 'the big city,' but it would've opened different doors. I'd hate to see you get stuck simply because it was the easiest route. You deserve to live a life that makes you happy. Not one that pleases everyone else. You only get this one."

3

Mia

DORIS' words haunt me all the way home. Home, where I am greeted by Steven vegging on the couch and a messy kitchen. Realizing he ate the leftovers I had been dreaming about all day, I pop a cup of mac and cheese into the microwave and tidy up.

After loading the dishwasher, I notice the dryer is open and instinctively know it isn't because he dried and put away the laundry I asked him to move over when he got home. Peeking inside the washer, I see it is still there and turn it on for another cycle.

Once I'm done eating my dinner over the sink, I head into the living room. Sitting on the opposite side of the couch, he gives me a nod of acknowledgement before his gaze returns to the basketball game on the TV.

"Hey," I greet.

"Hey. When did you get back?"

"About twenty minutes ago. I see you finished off the rest of the food from yesterday."

"Yeah. I didn't feel like going to the store. Sorry, did you want some?"

"I thought I'd heat some up for dinner, but it's fine." It's not fine. I'd been thinking about that casserole all day, but there is no point in saying that now.

"How was your day?" I ask instead of complaining.

"Good. Had the kids watch a movie today." His gaze hasn't left the screen since this conversation began. It's not lost on me that he doesn't ask anything about me when we sit in silence for a solid three minutes.

"My day was good," I express, hoping to prompt him.

"That's cool."

Heaving a sigh, I stand up from the couch, deciding tonight is better spent lost in a fantasy world. When I am almost to the bedroom, Steven calls from behind me, "Can you grab me another beer from the garage? We're out inside."

I'm not sure what it is about this request that triggers me, but this is the moment I break.

"No, Steven. I can't get you a beer," I yell, rushing back into the room. "All I do is get you things. I give and I give and I give and you do nothing in return. You couldn't even save me any hash brown casserole for dinner, knowing it's my favorite and that I hid that extra serving in the fridge."

Steven stares back at me, eyes wide. I've never yelled at him like this before. I've always been a sweet, docile partner, but something has woken up the animal in me.

"Geez, I'll get my own beer, then," he replies, moving to get up.

"This isn't about the beer," I clip back.

"Then what is it about? Because I've got no fucking clue.

You come in all hot as if I've done something wrong when I haven't done anything."

"That's exactly it. You haven't done anything. Not around the house. Not in our relationship. Not to get us closer to the ever-moving goal posts you set for our future."

"Whoa. Where is this all coming from?" he questions, hands up in surrender. "Did Rory say something to you at Thanksgiving? I swear, every time you two are together, you get on my case about shit after. I don't like you talking to her."

"You don't like me talking to my sister-in-law? And no, this isn't about anything she said. This is about me, wondering why I am living a life I don't want."

"What's that supposed to mean? You know we can't afford all the fancy shit they do. We're saving up for a house."

"Are we? Because you were quick to buy that new gaming console so you could play the latest college football game with your buddies. You didn't have a care in the world about our budget when you added that lift kit to your truck last year."

Frustrated, I sink into the chair in the corner of the room, head in my hands. "This isn't about money, Steven. It's about wanting to move forward in life. I want to get married while my Nonna is still around to see it. I want to have kids while my parents are young enough to enjoy them. I want to move forward in my life, and it feels as if we are stuck here in a never-ending loop."

"I can't control the housing market, Mia. What do you want from me?"

"You can control when you ask me to marry you," I shoot back. "You've been dangling the engagement carrot in front of my face for years now. Do you even have a ring?"

He shifts uncomfortably, and I know he doesn't. After a decade together and years of promising 'soon,' he's got nothing. I should have known that, but the confirmation cuts deep.

"I want a date, Steven."

"Fine. We can go to the movies next weekend?"

"Not a date. *A date*," I seeth. "A date for when we're getting engaged. I don't want to wait anymore."

"Next year, for sure," he replies.

"No, this year. By Chrsitmas," I retort.

"By Christmas?! There's no way we can get engaged in a month. Between Jeremy's bachelor party, the wrestling tournament, and all the holiday festivities, there isn't any time to get a ring and plan a proposal."

His refusal isn't what makes the record scratch in my brain. It's the other thing he said.

"Jeremy's bachelor party?" I echo calmly. That calm should send warning signs his way, but he doesn't heed them.

"I told you about this weeks ago," he sighs, as if his forgetful girlfriend taxes him. His body language tells a different story. He's puffing out his chest to make himself seem larger, more confident, but he won't meet my stare.

"I would remember that considering we agreed on no bachelor/bachelorette parties after you begged me not to go to Misty's."

"I didn't beg," he grumbles. "And this is different. Jeremy's my cousin. I have to go."

"And Misty is my best friend. I was her maid of honor, for Chrissake. You aren't even in Jeremy's wedding."

"I can't tell them my girlfriend won't let me go to bachelor parties, Mia. It's just going to make you seem controlling," he tries to reason. "I'll only be gone for three days and I'll be on my best behavior. We can talk more about this engagement stuff when I get back on Monday."

"You leave tomorrow?!" A nod is his only response.

"Where's the party, Steven. If it's in town, you shouldn't need to be gone at all."

"It's—I—"

"Because that was your biggest issue with Misty's party, right? That we'd be at a spa in Austin. You didn't want me to be that far away from you. And you were afraid she'd have some 'cowboy strippers' come and you'd consider that cheating. So his party must be at a cabin in the middle of nowhere. And y'all will only be fishing and drinking, right?"

"Well—I—no—"

"Where. Is it. Steven?" I ask again.

"Vegas." He winces, awaiting my response. Instead of blowing up as he expects, I shoot up and leave the room. I'm not mature enough to keep from slamming the door, though.

Pacing around my bedroom, I can't believe Steven would do this. Although, truthfully, I can. It is just like him to expect me to live under different rules than he does. Being a man somehow gives him special license to do what I can't. And why wouldn't he think that? I've never proven him any different. My family certainly acts that way. The women do everything while the men are simply there. I love my dad and uncles, but it is total BS.

When I get to the bed, I slide down to the floor and hug my knees, trying to fight the sensation of the walls closing in on me. When I finally regain my composure, I wipe away my tears. From this position, I am level with Steven's suitcase.

Taking a quelling breath, I come to a decision about my life. Screw getting engaged by Christmas. Screw waiting around forever for a life that isn't coming. A life I don't know if I actually want. This trip, this lack of consideration, is the final straw. Reaching for my phone, I know exactly what I have to do.

4

Mia

"Ladies and gentlemen, on behalf of myself and crew, we want to welcome you to Vancouver, where the local weather is a chilly six degrees Celsius. That is about forty-two for all the Americans on the flight. We thank you for choosing to fly with us and wish you luck if you're traveling further."

While the pilot finishes his closing remarks, I pull out my phone and power it back on. It took two hours after my call with Hadley to decide that I could no longer live my life on other people's terms. The only person who was going to save me was myself. Twenty-four hours after that, my bags were packed and I was ready to get started with the rest of my life.

As expected, there are several texts waiting for me from Steven. When he got back from his bachelor party last night and read my note, he freaked out. Having planned for that, I was already at Misty's. She and her husband graciously agreed to drive me to the airport. My ex has given up asking where I am and is now trying to guilt trip me into coming back with empty promises. Little does he know, his words have no more power over me.

A part of me wonders if I'm taking the coward's way out. Should I have given Steven the chance to live up to the ultimatum I gave him? I thought marrying him was what I wanted, but once I decided to leave, I was overtaken by a sense of relief. Maybe I should have stayed to tell him face-to-face, but I think sometimes to run is the brave thing.

Deciding the only way to truly get a fresh start is to cut him off entirely, I block his number and delete our years-long text thread. I wait for the panic to set in that I've made what feels like such a permanent step, but it never comes. Exhaling a sigh of relief, I send a message to Rory and Tony to let them know I've arrived safely to Canada, and then open a text from Hadley.

HADLEY

> When you land at YVR, there will be someone there to pick you up. We usually run a shuttle once a day based on the common international flights, but you're our only arrival this evening.

> Go ahead and settle in tonight and we can hit the ground running tomorrow morning.

Thank goodness for that. I was not looking forward to figuring out how to make it the two-hour drive to Sugar Peak by myself. The only other times I've traveled by myself, it was to visit my brother and my small town didn't have any ridesharing options.

Grabbing my carry-on from the overhead bin, I am practically giddy with anticipation. This is it! Once I step off this plane, I will no longer be on American soil. Life as I know it is about to change. Hopefully for the better.

Stepping out of the truck, I get my first gulp of mountain air. It's not as if the air in Trummings was stuffy or polluted by any means. It was the opposite, in fact. But something about the breeze around me feels different—aside from the obvious decrease in temperature. It feels new. It feels free. But that might simply be me.

As I revel in the sense of freedom, my luggage is plopped down beside me, causing me to startle.

"Sorry, I didn't mean to scare ya."

"My fault, my head was up in the clouds," I reply to the kind man Hadley sent to fetch me from the airport. "Thank you so much for the ride, Mr. Carlson."

He waves me off when I try to hand him some cash. "Call me Kevin. And don't sweat it. Your employer took care of paying for my gas and my time. They're taking good care of us. We townies may have been skeptical at first, but the resort is focused on supporting our local economy as much as they can. Hired a lot of local folks and give us discounts on their fancy amenities."

"I appreciate it nonetheless."

"If you want to pay me back, make sure you meet my girl, Megan. She needs a nice friend like you." Kevin has lived in Sugar Peak all his life. He and his wife were high school sweethearts. They have two kids, Adam and Megan, the resort's marketing manager. He insisted I meet her. He also insisted I take peanut butter cookies his wife sent from her diner. Too nervous to eat, I slipped them in my coat pocket when he was focused on the road.

"I can't wait to meet her. I'm sure we'll be working closely together," I reply. "Have a safe drive back into town!"

With a wave, I grab my suitcase and duffle bag—everything I could easily pack in two days' notice—and head inside the large wooden doors. The lobby is a perfect mix of modern luxury and classic Alps vibes. Unsure of where to go, I head to the front desk.

I am greeted by one of the most stunning women I have ever seen. She's all wild red curls, mocha skin, and hazel eyes that sparkle as she watches me approach. There is an almost magical quality about her.

"Hi, I'm Sunny. Checking in?"

"Sort of? I work here. Or I do tomorrow. Today I need help finding my room."

"You must be Mia! It's so nice to meet you," she singsongs. "Hadley told me you were starting today and I couldn't wait to meet you."

She offers me a smile so full of kindness that I find myself entranced. Of course she has the sunshiney demeanor that makes me immediately want to be her best friend. As someone who naturally fades into the background, I envy that.

"Give me a moment and I will ping Megan for you. She can show you to your accommodations."

"Thank you, Sunny."

"It's my pleasure. Feel free to grab yourself a hot chocolate from the cafe while you wait. Tell them it's your first day and it's on the house!"

Taking my cue to leave the desk, I survey the lobby before me. Even though it's only the first of December, no expense has been spared decorating it for the holidays. I can already see spaces to set up a few of the events Hadley sent over on her spreadsheet. The woman is detailed, I'll give her that. I'm happy to take this stress off her plate.

As I turn away from the massive fir by the window, something connects to my knees, causing them to buckle. My unfulfilling life flashes before my eyes as I fall toward the pristine wooden floors. Before I connect with the ground, an arm wraps around my waist, holding me up.

In this position, neither my head nor feet are on the ground as I dangle in a pair of strong arms. As whoever grabs me makes a move to straighten me, a large, furry head appears under my stomach, snout sniffing my pockets. Finding what he was after, the dog sticks his entire face into my coat. I buck at the motion, and both me and my savior go toppling over.

Somehow in the fall, I end up straddling one of the hottest men I have ever seen. The moment my eyes lock into his and my hands plant on his firm chest, the world around me freezes.

One of the casualties of being in a long-term relationship is appreciating how attractive other people can be. I always hated when Steven's eyes wandered, so I made sure to never do the same. Nothing cuts the way hearing "the love of your life" wax poetic about Margot Robbie when you are her physical opposite. I made it a point not to mention or leer at hot guys, and somewhere along the line it became not noticing them all together.

Clearly that habit ended with my relationship because I cannot look away from this man. He's a perfect mix of Jenson Ackles, Chad Michael Murray, and every mountain man living in my Kindle. I don't know what set this man walked off, but I am going to be streaming that show.

I'm so enraptured staring at him, I don't notice how weird it must be until something sloppy and wet touches the side of my face, pulling me back into the moment. The moment where I am straddling a very hot stranger in a very public hotel lobby.

"Oh my gosh, I am so sorry," I rush out as I quickly stand up.

"Don't you worry about it, sweetheart," the man I was just plastered to drawls. "It's my fault more than yours. Well, it's my dog's fault, but I suppose I am responsible for his actions since I'm the one who trained him. Not that you'd think he had any training with the way he went after you."

Dog...? Right. Glancing around, I spot the pooch in question, sitting beside his owner's head. With more grace than I'm sure I had, the man jumps up from the floor and dusts himself off. Wiping his hand down the front of his shirt, he offers it to me.

"Seeing as we gave this lobby a show, I think I at least owe you an introduction. I'm Jamie. This troublemaker is Crosby."

"Mia," I say a little too breathily. I want to blame it on the whole rolling around on the floor thing, but truthfully, it's because his light brown eyes have my darker ones entranced

"Hi, Mia. I apologize for the tumble. I'm sure we can find a way to compensate for the—"

"That's okay," I interrupt. "Accidents happen."

"Still, we can't have guests being accosted in the lobby." He says this to me, but his glare cuts to the large dog, who shows no signs of guilt. He simply wags at the attention.

"It's fine. I promise. And I'm not a guest. I work here. Or will, at least, starting tomorrow. I'm the new events manager."

5

JAMIE

Fᴜᴄᴋ ᴍᴇ. The pretty little thing Crosby and I nearly took out works here? I can't decide if that's a good thing or a bad thing. On the one hand, the fact that she didn't freak out leads me to believe she will be pleasant to work with. God knows we need the help. Hadley has been stressed to the max trying to replace all the positions that left when the old manager bailed.

On the other hand, having a coworker who embodies my wet dreams is going to be a huge challenge. I can still feel the way her thighs felt around my hips. A perfect fit. Thankfully, she got up before I could make us both uncomfortable. More uncomfortable than accosting a stranger anyway.

Speaking of our crash collision, the cause of the chaos boops my hand. Crouching down, I ruffle the mangy mutt's hair before chastising him. "You can't go rubbing up on a lady

22

just because you think she's pretty. I raised you better than that."

He tilts his head as if he's contemplating it, even though I know he has no idea what I'm saying.

"I think he was after this," a sweet voice pipes in from behind me. Peering up, I see her holding out a peanut butter cookie that resembles the ones Vicki serves at the diner.

"Vicki's?" I ask.

"Yes! How did you know? Kevin gave it to me, but I was too nervous to eat it. He can have it, if that's okay."

What would she have to be nervous about? The new job? I've only been around her for a few minutes, but I can tell she's going to be great at it. I may try to avoid them most of the time, but I know people. Working the types of jobs I do, I often get a peek behind the curtain of who most people really are. This girl, though—she is definitely all sugar, spice, and everything nice.

Crosby nudges me as if he understands a cookie was offered to him and I haven't accepted it on his behalf yet.

"Sure," I sigh. "But know once you give him that, you'll be his new best friend. Get ready to see a lot of him. I try to keep him out of the guest spaces, but we were out on a walk when I got a call from Lars that he needed something fixed in the kitchen."

"I take it that means you aren't a guest either."

"Shit, sorry. I guess I didn't finish our introduction. I'm the head of maintenance around here. If something's broken, I fix it."

Her eyes glint with mirth as she asks, "And Crosby carries the tool box?" It's fucking cute, and I can't help myself from flirting back.

"Nah. He serves as a good wingman when there are beautiful women around, though."

She blushes when I wink at her, and I almost keep going before I remember that this woman is my coworker. As in, a woman I will be spending time around. In the past, I haven't minded getting together with coworkers since I'm only there for the season, but I've taken a permanent role at Sugar Peak Resort. I need to at least find out if she's single before I shoot my shot. Because with hips and a smile like hers, I want one.

Rising back to my full height, I don't notice how she appears to be the perfect height to rest her head on my shoulder and I really really don't notice where that head hits when she gets on her knees to offer Crosby the cookie.

I glance around the lobby, trying not to scowl at the holiday decorations that have been set up in the past couple weeks. Struggling to come up with a conversation topic, I'm saved by the bell when Megan shows up.

"Hi, Jamie! Hi, Crosb— Oh, you must be Mia," she greets, turning her attention to my now standing companion.

"I am. It's nice to meet you, Megan. I must confess, I feel like I know you already."

"I have one of those faces," she remarks. "Everyone swears they know me."

"You do resemble a girl that was in my high school math class, but that isn't why. Your father drove me here from the airport and he basically read me your biography. I hope the story about getting your braces stuck in your bikini top and flashing everyone at your family reunion wasn't a secret. Based on his delivery, that is not the first time he's told it."

"Ugh, dammit, Kevin. It's not a secret, considering twenty Carlsons and sixteen Jansons saw it, but it isn't the first impression I want to make on new friends." Megan groans. "I see you've met the resort's eye candy."

Mia freezes and glances up at me. Does that mean she

thinks I'm eye candy? I can't say I'm mad if she does. I certainly return the sentiment.

"Crosby, here, is a favorite with all the ladies."

"Oh. Um, yes, I have," Mia stammers.

"He introduced himself to her earlier trying to get one of your mom's cookies. Took us both out," I supply.

Megan laughs. "I can't say I blame him. My brother and I have definitely come to blows over the last one before. I'd say Crosby has good taste, but he likes Spencer, so I'm not sure how true that is."

"Spencer?" Mia asks.

"He's the ski lift operator. I'm sure you'll see him around. He's pretty to look at, but not much going on up here," Megan explains.

"Careful, Meg. Someone might think you don't loathe him if they hear you complimenting him."

"As if," she scoffs. "There's not enough booze at Dirty Dick's to make that man palatable. Anyway, I need to get our new friend here to her room so she can get unpacked and rested to meet with ring master Hadley tomorrow. Bye, boys."

"Bye, Megan. Bye, Mia. It was nice to meet you. I'm sure I'll see you around."

"I'm sure you will. Have a good night." She gives Crosby a pat before following Megan down the hall toward the closest exit to the staff housing.

At that moment, my walkie talkie crackles and I hear the angry voice of head baker, Lars.

After taking care of Lars' very much not emergent issue, I trudge back to my cabin. Located on the opposite side of the resort from the staff housing, it's a quaint two-room chalet with a beautiful view of the mountain. Since unlike most of the staff, I am not seasonal, Thiago offered the cabin up as part of my work agreement.

I jumped at the chance to have some distance from the rest of the staff. It's not that I don't like people. I do. I've had a lot of jobs where working with people was my main focus—hiking guide, camp counselor—but after a long day, it's nice to have a place to call my own where I don't have to worry about hearing noises from my neighbors. Plus, Crosby would hate being stuck in a hotel room all day.

Leaving my boots and coat by the door, I rifle through the mail I picked up from Sunny and check the dinner I put in the crockpot. It has another thirty minutes before it's ready to eat. That's another perk of the cabin. Unlike the staff rooms, it has a full kitchen, not just a kitchenette. I may not be the greatest chef, but I enjoy making food for myself that doesn't come straight from a microwave.

Most of the mail in question is from the resort, but a post-card catches my attention. My stomach knots, knowing the familiar handwriting that will greet me when I flip it over.

Enjoying the breeze while you enjoy the freeze.
Congratulations on the job and hello from Mexico.
- Merry Christmas, Mom

Every month or so, I receive a card like this from my mother, featuring whatever sunny locale she and Dad are at now. Always nomads, my parents met working one summer at a lodge on Lake Superior. Very much not against coworker co-mingling, they got together and spent a few years traveling from lodge to lodge. I was born a few years later, once they kept their stints to years-long instead of months long.

Growing up, it was awesome getting to experience so much of what Canada has to offer, rich city girls on vacation included, but it was hard to make and keep friends when I never knew when we'd pick up and move next. Once I turned eighteen and finished secondary school, they decided to go back to their nomadic ways and signed up to work on a ship. Now they travel all over the world, one cruise at a time.

I took after them more than I would have thought, working odd jobs and traveling with the seasons. This position at Sugar Peak is the first role without an end date I've ever taken. I was apprehensive at first, but they made me an offer I couldn't refuse. Plus, at thirty-three, I'm starting to crave the roots I never had.

It's funny to read her give a holiday greeting, seeing as they were never big in our house. They were typically busy serving guests wherever we were. My parents bucked at most traditions, holidays included. If I was lucky, the resort would have a kids' party they could sneak me into.

The lack of emphasis stuck with me. One scan of my barren cabin, you'd never guess we were a few short weeks from Santa's big day. I never saw the point of adding decor you're going to have to take down in a month. And aside from a few girlfriends in my younger years, I never had anyone I needed to exchange gifts with. Plus, like my parents, I am usually working on Christmas.

Taking Mom's card, I add it to the dresser drawer where I keep the rest. They don't hold any sentimental value for me, but I can't seem to throw them out. Maybe they remind me of the dreams I have. As much as I enjoy my life, seasonal jobs don't allow much room for saving up. Because of that, I've not traveled much outside of Canada, aside from a trek to Detroit—it was okay—and New York—way too crowded and loud.

The retention bonus I'll receive after completing a full year at the lodge is the push I need to have saved enough to take my dream vacation to Costa Rica. All the things I hope to do on that trip filter through my mind. This time, a new image emerges of long dark waves across my chest as I lay in a hammock, staring at the ocean.

Shaking off the weird new addition, I head into my room to grab a quick shower before my roast is ready. There'll be plenty of time to daydream once I'm warm and clean.

6

Mia

At 8:15 a.m. there's a sharp knock on my door. Pulling it open, I'm surprised to see Hadley greeting me with a cup of coffee and a stressed smile.

"Good morning," she greets. "I thought I would walk you to the office this morning and give you a tour on the way."

"That would be great," I reply. "Megan gave me a mini tour last night, but it was too dark to see much."

"That's what I figured."

"Thank you for the coffee. It's exactly how I like it."

"Good, I'm glad," she replies warmly.

"None for you?"

"I've already had a cup this morning. I try to make it to at least nine before drinking a second."

"What time do you get up?"

"Usually around 6:30 a.m. I know you won't normally start until later in the morning, but since we have a lot of paperwork to get through, I figured it was best to get a jump on it. I know you're eager to get planning and time is of the essence."

She's not wrong there. I'd had the nursing home holiday party planned since before Halloween. A resort of this magnitude with a range of guests filtering in and out, I'll have a lot more to manage. I'm up for the task, though.

As we walk, Hadley points out some of the rooms Megan showed me yesterday. The staff housing is connected to the main lodge through a heated breezeway. Thank goodness for that. I can't imagine how cold it would be at night without it.

The breezeway connects at the gift shop, which is adjoined with the casual bar and restaurant. When you get to the main structure, you're greeted by a large lounge, lobby, and cafe. On the other side is a fine dining Brazilian steakhouse and more guest rooms that mirror the ones connected to the shop. Behind each side of guest rooms are hot tubs and saunas, that the staff can also use if they are free.

As I take in the lounge, I have to work to keep my jaw off the floor. It was gorgeous last night with the tall fireplaces and twinkly lights, but nothing beats the view during the day. Floor to ceiling windows show off a breathtaking mountain landscape that reminds you why you're here. I went skiing a few times with my family as a child, and several more at my friend Trevor's cabin in Michigan, but this place is giving him a run for his NFL money.

"This elevator is just for staff. It connects directly to the offices. There's one on the other side that goes to the other guest amenities, including the theater room, library, gym, spa, and game room. I am sure you'll be utilizing many of these areas for your events. Once we get your paperwork done, we can take a peek. You'll need your badge to get access to those areas, which I will give you once we get into the office."

As the doors open, we enter the office area. I can't help but be impressed. Being on the second floor and built into a hill, I expected them to be dark and dingy. But like the rest of the resort, they have both a modern and rustic vibe that is polished yet perfect for the setting.

Turning to the right, she leads me into a nice sized office. Sitting behind a desk, she grabs a stack of papers in an envelope.

"Inside here is your badge. I need you to fill out all of this paperwork so that we can file everything with the proper authorities, and start your employment officially."

Her tone is warm but all business. Something tells me that while Hadley is kind, she could use a little more fun in her life. I fill out my paperwork, and she continues to give me the lay of the land, discussing other team members, her and Thiago's schedules, and what events they have run so far. Once I finish, we head a few doors down to an office with two desks. A familiar face is seated behind one of them.

"Hi, Mia!" she exclaims.

"Hello," I greet in return.

"Thank you for taking care of her yesterday, Megan. I know you're excited to get events off your plate so you can focus more on the marketing side of things."

"No problem. I was happy to help. And very happy to pass off the executing. I'm looking forward to posting and attending."

"Wonderful," Hadley replies. "I'll let you two get to work. Thiago will probably drop by at some point to say 'hello.' Otherwise, I will leave you to it. Megan can give you access to the company card and make connections as needed. She's not only one of the employees who stuck around, but she is local so she knows everyone. Don't hesitate to text or call me should you need anything."

I give her my thanks before she heads back into her office, not without getting that post 9 a.m. coffee fix.

Megan and I make small talk for a few minutes before I dig through the files. I did some research on the plane to understand what events similar resorts are doing to make sure we are giving people the experience they expect. It's a mix of large, resort-wide events and smaller 'come as you may' events for different groups. Thankfully, I have access to the guest logs so I know the ages and number of kids at the resort at any given time.

"Megan, do you mind if I run my schedule for the next month with you? I'd love to get your opinion before I start making plans."

Looking up from her phone, Megan gives me her full attention. "Of course! I need a break from editing social media videos anyway."

"Here's what I am thinking. Once a day, I will host a small social event where guests can mingle and meet each other. Some events will be for all ages, while others will be more selective. Then we have the large holiday celebrations that happen at the end of the month."

"Sounding good so far. What are some of the options?"

"Happy hour, of course, a game tournament of some kind—could change weekly based on ages—gingerbread house decorating, trivia night, and themed ice skating nights. I've also thought about a holiday craft, hot cocoa bar, Mahjong tournament, and holiday movie night."

"Those are all fantastic and easy to throw together quickly," she replies, but her face is pensive.

"What?"

"What? Nothing. They'll all be hits, I'm sure."

"Your face says differently."

"Dammit! My face is always giving me away. It's why my brother always beats me at poker. Oh, poker! That could be a fun idea. A casino night."

"Adding it to the list. But you're not getting away with not answering my question."

"Fine," she sighs. "Maybe it's the small town girl in me, or maybe it's an American thing, but what the hell is Mahjong?"

I can't help but bust out laughing at Megan's puzzled expression. That wasn't the objection I thought she'd have. Once I contain my giggles, I formulate a response. "Trust me. You can't come from a smaller town than me. Mahjong is a tile-based game created in China centuries ago. It was something the older ladies at the nursing home I worked at loved to play. In the last year or so, it has become popular in affluent circles, but if it isn't big here, I don't want to confuse people. It can be a hard game to master."

"I think you should do it. It might be fun to watch some snotty rich ladies pretend they know what something is simply because it's supposed to be fancy. Plus, it sounds exotic."

"Alright, we'll keep it. Now for the big events. Hadley let me know that we are planning a big party at the end of the month to celebrate the New Year. Since we have the big feast on the twenty-fifth, I was thinking we could start the festivities on the twenty-seventh and go through the first."

"What about Boxing Day?"

"Boxing Day?"

"The day after Christmas. You can't have nothing planned for Boxing Day!"

"You think people will want to celebrate on the twenty-sixth after big events on Christmas Eve and Christmas Day?"

"Of course they will, it's Boxing Day!" Megan looks almost offended, so I nod my head thoughtfully while subtly searching 'Boxing Day' into my browser. I've heard the day after Christmas called that before, but I didn't realize it was *a thing.*

"Mia, are you googling 'Boxing Day' right now?"

"Maybe..."

She huffs out a laugh and rolls her chair over to mine. "What does it say?"

"It says it's a day to spend with family and shop deals. It also says people get off work. Why would you need to shop deals when you just gave everyone presents? And if people are off work, who is manning the shops?"

"Think of it as Canada and the UK's Black Friday."

"But Black Friday is for Christmas gifts."

"And this is to spend Christmas gift cards and return the horrible sweater your Aunt Angelique got you."

Taking in her suggestion, I think about how guests would want to spend this holiday after the holidays. I assume they are over big feasts by now and they can't do a lot of shopping up the mountain. Then it comes to me. Kevin mentioned how much the resort has supported the town, and I thought of another way they can do so, but I am going to need Megan's connections.

"I've got it. How about we start the day with some winter games up the mountain and then down here we can host a crafts fair where local artisans, bakers, and craftsmen can sell locally made goods to the guests?"

Megan freezes momentarily as she considers it. "That is an amazing idea!"

"It's going to be hard to pull off. Do you think you can get the townspeople on board?"

"Absolutely, that will be an easy sell. Why don't we go down to Dirty Dick's for Ladies' Night later this week and we can start pitching the idea?"

Megan and I spend the rest of the morning brainstorming and getting everything we need ready to pitch Thiago and the town. It will be a big undertaking, but I think it is the perfect way to kick off the week's festivities until the New Year.

7

Mia

After a long first day, I am both invigorated and worn out. I had several meetings with the staff today to discuss how they can help support events, including one with a head baker who could not be less enthused to help with gingerbread houses. Megan assures me that it is simply Lars' face and he doesn't hate me. I'm not convinced.

After hours of traipsing around the resort, including a trip up the mountain to scout locations, the soaker tub in my room is calling my name. I was pleasantly surprised to discover it last night. I expected staff accommodations to be meager at best, but they are better than any place in Trummings. I'm sure the guest rooms are more extravagant, but this studio is all I need. It has a small kitchenette and even a sitting area, so I don't have to live on my bed.

I sink into the couch with a glass of "welcome to the team"

wine to sip on before rallying to start the bath. As I decompress, I pull out my phone for the first time in hours. Fifteen minutes of mindless scrolling is just what the doctor ordered.

My video showing me how to tame my thick curls into something more manageable is interrupted by an incoming text.

RORY

I've been thinking…

Sounds dangerous. I'm guessing about me and not an amazing new business concept to wow your investors.

You would be correct.

Do you remember when you came for your birthday last spring and we drank so many espresso martinis Tony had to pick us up and we stayed awake until dawn?

For my thirtieth birthday last year, Tony and Rory flew me out to visit them. I'd seen them during our annual Michigan trip, but we didn't get much one on one time as we were trying to get Zade's fake girlfriend to fall in real love with him.

Since Steven had a wrestling tournament that weekend, I went solo. Rory and I drank enough vodka to be considered Russian and then spent the next day hungover at a fancy spa, sweating it out in the sauna.

Remember is a stretch. But it sounds vaguely familiar.

Valid. One thing I do remember about it is you lamenting a certain terrible ex boyfriend's insufficiencies in the pleasure department.

OMG

I choke on my sip of wine reading her response. Now on top of being embarrassed about my sex life, I have to be mortified hearing about my brother's.

It wasn't that Steven was bad in bed. I mean, he wasn't great, but he was okay. Sometimes. It's that he lacked imagination and effort. I was young and inexperienced when we got together, so everything was new and exciting. Until it wasn't.

The man had three go-to positions and anytime I suggested something outside of them, you would think I went on the news and announced he wasn't a man. I asked him to talk dirty to me once, even showing him examples that I enjoyed reading. He told me he "respected me too much to talk to me that way." If only he respected me enough to reciprocate head.

Make a list! A naughty list if you want to be
seasonal about it. Write down all the things
you want to explore and then find a hot
Canadian Mountie to help you check
them off.

I'm not hooking up with a Mountie.

Why not! They have to have good stamina to
ride those horses and that uniform…

Actually, if you find any of those for sale, send
me the link

Barf.

Come on. It will be fun. I can help if you want.
I have some *very* creative ideas.

I'll think about it. For now, I'm going to soak
in the tub.

Have a very PG night with my brother.

Have fun! Don't put tub stuff on the list. It's
like asking the universe for a UTI.

Goodnight, Aurora!

Heading into the bathroom to start my bath, I turn on the
tap and take off my makeup while I wait for it to warm up.
Once it's the perfect temperature, I add in my body wash as
temporary bubbles and make a note to order bath supplies.
Megan mentioned the pharmacy in town makes their own bath
bombs and salt kits. I'll have to text my friend Molly and ask
her favorites. No one loves a bath more than her.

Leaning my head against the lip of the tub, tension leaks
from my muscles. It's as if years—not days—of stress are leaving
my body. Stress I didn't know I was holding. I never realized
how heavy a weight my relationship was until I freed myself

from it. I let go of the guilt of never putting myself first, regrets for missed opportunities, and shame of never being 'enough.' On this, the first night of my new life, I vow to make the most of the fresh start I've been given. Beginning with Rory's damn list.

As my brain whirls with ideas, it also replays my encounter with Jamie from earlier. A local bakery dropped off treats. When I joked with Megan that if every day was going to include pastries, I'd be making use of the gym sooner than I thought.

At that exact moment, Jamie entered the office. His gaze was physical weight down my body as he gave me a once-over. I expected him to make a cheesy comment about not needing to work out, but he said nothing. I don't know why I thought he'd be one to throw out cheap one-liners. Instead, he reached for a pastry of his own.

Seconds later, he turned to me and a cute smile graced his face. "You've got a little something," he commented, pointing to his cheek.

He chuckled as I rubbed my face. "Did I get it?"

Shaking his head, he reached forward to swipe at the cranberry filling. "Mmm, delicious," he hummed as he popped his thumb into his mouth for a taste. "Thanks for that. Now I was able to try both options." Then he walked away!

"I think I just ovulated," Megan said from our office doorway. I wanted to chastise her, but honestly, same.

Dealing with attraction to someone other than Steven is strange but not unwelcome. It's as if I had blinders on. I had no idea how many hot men were out and about in the world. To be fair, I've known most of the men in my town my entire life, so it's possible that I simply didn't find any of *them* attractive. But between Jamie, the guy I saw manning the bar during the lunch rush, and the ski instructor, it's eye candy galore.

Jamie is definitely the hottest, though. And not solely because I saw him in his tool belt fixing a piece of siding when I was up on the mountain earlier today. He has an aura about him that's attractive. He projects a sense of confidence and self-assurance. I don't know what it is about that, but it's working for me. So much so, that I was tempted to lick the cranberry filling off his thumb before he pulled that move. It took actual effort to hold back.

But damn was the show worth it. I spent a good ten minutes wondering what it would feel like to have those same lips on my skin instead of his finger.

Pulling myself out of my haze of lust, I realize my water has gone tepid and my fingers are pruny. I slip on the robe Rory bought me several Christmases ago. It isn't incredibly warm due to its length, but I'm convinced it's made with butterfly lashes; it's so soft. I return to my cozy spot on the couch after grabbing the resort notepad from the vanity desktop. My mind whirls with possibilities of what to include on the list. Hand necklaces, pierced partners, and role playing all filter through, but feel more advanced than I'm ready to tackle. I think it's best to keep it simple. I can always add more as I check items off.

I decide to give the list a holiday theme because I'm two glasses in and what's a better Christmas present to myself than this?

Mia's Naughty List

1. Jingle Bell Rock (oral)
2. Santa Claus is Comin' to Town (morning sex)
3. Underneath the Tree (bondage)

4. A Marshmallow World (food play)
5. My Favorite Things (incorporate a toy)
6. Sleigh Ride (get good at cowgirl)
7. Up on the Housetop (semi-public play)
8. Deck the Halls (wall sex)
9. Let It Snow (shower sex)
10. Holiday in the Sun (sex on the beach)

Part of me is ashamed of how basic some of the items on my list are. It highlights how unbalanced my relationship was that I couldn't ask for such simple things. Most men would be thrilled their partner wanted to spice things up.

Satisfied with what I have for now, I set the pad down and walk over to my balcony door. I want to get a final dose of the fresh mountain air before the last of the residual warmth from my bath leaves my skin. When I was little, I used to love running outside after a hot bath or shower and watching the steam radiate off me. I was also the queen of jumping from the hot tub into the pool. I'm no adrenaline junkie, but that shock to my system always invigorates me.

Staring off into the snowy peaks, I inhale one last gulp of cool air before pulling my door closed. Only it won't. It opened easily enough, but now it's locked in place. Tugging harder, I attempt to get it to budge but to no avail.

"No, no, no," I mutter to myself. "This is not good."

What should I do? I can't leave it open all night. It will wreck the heater and worse, leave me freezing. Of course this would happen to me. Panicked, I scan my room for anything I could use to leverage the door when I spot the welcome binder. Maybe there is a trick to shutting the door I missed.

Rushing over, I scan the pages, but nothing jumps out. Shit. Should I call the front desk? Flipping to the front, I see a red box that says, "In case of maintenance emergency, text (555-427-8801)." Hallelujah. It's something.

Shooting off a text to that number, I get a quick response requesting my room number. They let me know that someone will be over in twenty minutes. That's not too long. I consider reengaging in my mission to close the door but decide I could do more harm than good. I'll let the professional handle it.

8

Mia

INSTEAD OF PACING while I wait, I can at least be productive. Opening my closet, I pull out my suitcase. I unpacked my clothing and toiletries last night, but I left in some of the objects I brought to make the hotel room feel more like home.

I know I can't have my own tree as I usually would, but I still want to have some decorations. Grabbing the pack of five-foot lights, I twist them over the headboard of my bed. I wrap the lamp in tinsel garland and tape the excess above the two door frames. Beside the TV, I add the one decoration I couldn't leave behind: a nativity scene my Nonna gave me.

She and Papa got it on an Alaskan cruise before I was born. It features a parka-clad Mary and Joseph, bundled up baby Jesus, igloo for a barn, and a variety of arctic animals—seal, wolf, and moose—instead of wisemen. It is all set on a soft animal skin. I add another set of lights to the entertainment center, to strategically highlight the nativity scene.

Despite the lower temperature of the room, it feels festive once I finish my setup. Between the decorations, photos of my family, and a few small knickknacks, the room is much homier. I'm about to check my phone to get an update on the time when there is a light rap on the door.

Checking the peephole, I suck in a breath. I did not consider the person they'd send to fix my door would be the hot handyman. I should have. I was so relieved someone was coming to help, it didn't cross my mind. I do a final scan of the room to make sure I don't have anything unmentionable lying around.

"Hi," I greet as I open the door. His eyes widen for a moment as if he's also surprised to see me, but he schools his features quickly.

"I hear we have a stuck door?"

My cheeks heat and I stare anywhere but at his face when I mumble my affirmation. Stepping to the side, I allow him into my room. He lingers by me for a moment before walking to the door in question. When he does a survey of the room, I wonder how everything appears from an outsider perspective, especially when he grimaces.

"Something wrong?" I ask.

"Not at all. It's cozy in here."

"It is." I smile.

"No narwhal?"

"Huh?"

"In your nativity," he says. "Wasn't there a narwhal in that one claymation? I don't remember Jesus being there, but it's been a while."

"That's the beginning of *Elf*. I think the only Will Ferrell movie with baby Jesus is *Talladega Nights*."

"I'll have to take your word for it. I'm not big on Christmas."

"What?!" I gasp. My shock must register on my face because Jamie offers a sheepish smile in return.

Not 'big on Christmas?' What does that even mean? Holidays in the Ricci family are the biggest of deals. Not only do we do a traditional Christmas feast, but we have gatherings leading up to the big day. It is practically a month-long affair. This is the first year I won't be there to be part of the traditions. I couldn't even face my mom to tell her, choosing to text her on my way to the airport so she couldn't guilt me into staying.

Sensing my inner turmoil, Jamie turns his attention to the balcony door. Kneeling beside the opening, he brushes off the snow before fiddling with the track.

"I'm confused," I sputter out a moment later.

"About the door?"

"About Christmas."

Hand rubbing the back of his neck, he turns to glance at me as I step closer. "My family usually worked on Christmas. Now I work on Christmas. We exchanged presents and stuff but didn't make it a whole thing. I think you have more decorations in here than I've ever had in my life."

Whoa. If this meager display is a lot to him, I can't imagine what he'd think of the streets of Trummings. Residents try their hardest to outdo one another in their light displays. People save up for that December electricity bill all year long.

"But you've seen *Elf*?"

"'Seen' is a stretch, but it's been on in rooms the same time I was in them."

I don't even want to ask about the sacred film that is *Love Actually*.

"This appears to be rocking your world," he drawls, eyes twinkling with delight over his tipped lips.

"It is," I confess, bringing a hand to my chest. My bare chest. Because I am not in my pajamas, but the thin jersey robe I put on after my bath. Oh my God!

The motion brings Jamie's attention to the area, and I peer down in horror to see the cold from the open door has my nipples standing at attention. Mortification rolls through my body, chilling me far more than the outdoor temps. I've met this man twice. The first time I ended up straddling him. The second, I practically showed him my nips.

"I, um, am going to change into something... warmer. You don't need anything from me, do you?"

He clears his throat before meeting my gaze. "No, I'm good. Shouldn't be more than five minutes and then I'll get out of your hair."

Taking his word for it, I grab my pajamas and rush into the bathroom. The silk button-up sleep set unfortunately doesn't do much to hide my girls. When I return to the room, I pull the throw blanket off the bed and wrap it around my shoulders strategically.

Jamie is standing in the sitting area, door blessedly shut.

"You got it!"

"I did," he replies, hesitantly. I may have left the room the uncomfortable one, but now Jamie is the one shifting his weight and not meeting my eyes. "You should be all good now. I removed a rusty screw and put in a new one."

"Thank you. I promise not to need you again anytime soon," I tease in an attempt to lighten the mood, but it does little to change his energy.

"No worries if you do. I'll see myself out. Have a good night, Mia."

A shiver wracks through my body at the hoarse way he says my name, but he doesn't notice in his haste to exit. That was weird.

Did seeing the outline of my nipples make him that uneasy? Surely he's seen his fair share of them before. The man is gorgeous.

Deciding to rot in bed for the rest of the evening, I lean over to grab my wine glass. That's when I notice it. *Mia's Naughty List*. On the coffee table and in full fucking view of the room.

There's no way he saw it. He was several feet away fixing the door. But I was in the bathroom primping for a bit. And he wasn't next to the door when I came back.

Nope. No. He didn't see it. I am not putting that possibility into the universe because I would have to quit this job and probably walk out into the mountains and bury myself in the snow to escape the embarrassment.

9

JAMIE

MIA'S NAUGHTY LIST. Mia's fucking *Naughty List.* That's what has occupied my mind for the past few days. That, and all our encounters. No matter how many times I turn it over in my mind, it remains there. And I have questions. A lot of them.

Why did she make the list? Are these all things she hasn't done or things she wants to do again during the holidays? If the former, what kind of losers has she been with? How did she determine what to put on the list? How does she plan on completing it? Who does she plan on completing it with? Can I throw my hat in the ring?

Seeing the list moments after coming face-to-face with her sexy body in that thin robe had all kinds of scenarios popping into my brain. I thought about offering to help with her list right then. Every item. It would take all night, but it would have been worth it.

I thought if I slept on it, I would come to the conclusion that it is a bad idea to get involved with her, but that isn't the case. If anything, I want it more. I haven't figured out how to approach it. Normally, I would cut straight to the chase, but I have a suspicion that would scare her off.

From what I've gathered seeing her around the resort the past few days and what I gleaned from conversations with Megan, she moved here after a breakup. She's probably looking for a rebound, which is perfect for me. We both have a good time and she goes back home—because a sweet, small town girl like her always ends up back home—with an idea of what she likes and deserves from a sexual partner. Hopefully, it will stop her from going back to whatever schmuck lost her in the first place. I may not be a relationship guy, but if I was, I would be smart enough not to lose a girl like Mia.

I don't know anything about her ex, but the fact that he wasn't kneeling at this goddess' feet, taking her any way he could have her is mind-blowing to me. Now I have to convince her to give me the chance to blow hers right back.

When Megan lets it slip that she is taking Mia to Dirty Dick's for Ladies' Night, I know I have to be there. No way am I going to give anyone else a chance to shoot their shot. She'll end up with some one-pump chump who maybe checks off an item or two and then bails. I'm ready to commit to checking off as many items as possible for as long as she's here.

It doesn't take much convincing to get Spencer to join me at the bar. He's always trolling for a good time. He would probably be a good option to assist Mia, but I'm not sure he has the emotional maturity to finesse the situation. Plus, I saw her first. Childish? Maybe. But all's fair in love and sex or however the saying goes.

Physically, Mia is my dream girl. She's all soft curves, long dark hair, and olive skin. It was hard to tell when she had her coat on what was underneath, but her robe and pajamas painted a picture that had my mouth watering to worship her.

"Hey, guys," Brooks, one of the bartenders at Dirty Dick's, greets. "What can I get you?"

"I'll take a Coors," I reply while Spencer opts for a Jack and Coke.

"I'm surprised you wanted to come out tonight," my friend states. "I've only gotten you to come out a few times and never at your request."

"What can I say? I have a good feeling."

He searches my face for something, but he doesn't find it. I do have a good feeling about tonight. Mainly because I plan to proposition Mia, but he doesn't need to know that.

"A little birdy told me you had quite the run-in with the new event manager the other day," he drops casually.

I take a pull of my beer to keep from snapping at him. I opt for a more chill reaction. "Where'd you hear that from? I know it wasn't Megan—she can't stand you—and no one else was there."

"First of all, Megan loves me. She simply hides that love in layers of sass and digs."

"Layers and layers and layers and—" I murmur.

"Okay, I get it. She's not my biggest fan. But now that we work together, I'm determined to bring her around. No woman can resist my charm. And if that doesn't work, I have other methods of convincing."

My eyebrow shoots up at that admission. I was simply trying to deflect. Though it is funny how much Megan appears to dislike Spencer. Most people love him, so there has to be more to the story. They both grew up here, so it's possible they have a history I don't know about.

"And what methods are those, Spence?"

"Her mother, of course." The sip of beer I took goes down

the wrong pipe and I choke so hard other customers turn to glare at me. Apparently my almost dying is louder than the playlist that has been the same for thirty years.

"Damn, that isn't where my mind went at all. And also, what?" I finally manage to sputter. That is not the direction I thought he was taking that. Mia's dirty bucket list has put my mind permanently in the gutter.

"Vicki loves me. Always has. She viewed me as a good influence on her son, Adam."

"Ah, so she doesn't know you at all."

Spencer gasps. "Take that back. I'm a very good boy."

"I don't think there is a soul on this earth who believes that's true," a feminine voice quips from behind us. Turning around, I spot Megan ready to square off.

"You know that isn't true, Meggy. There are a lot of women who would be more than willing to attest to what a good boy I am. You're simply jealous you aren't one of them. I get it."

"You wish. You wouldn't even have to wait for Adam to rip your balls off if you tried. I'd beat him to it."

He winces at the mention of his best friend. Something tells me he has a lot to do with the tension between these two.

"Whatever. You come here alone, Tink?" he asks, changing the subject.

"No, Mia is with me."

"Is Mia your invisible friend?" He makes a show of exaggeratedly searching around Megan, who is standing alone.

"No." She rolls her eyes. "She went to the bathroom."

We both grimace at that. Dirty Dick's is a fine place to drink, but it's best patronized if you don't touch anything. Or breathe too deeply. It definitely isn't a place any resort guests would want to be caught dead at. They're better off staying on property than venturing to this hole in the wall.

"I tried to warn her," she agrees. "It's a lesson we all must learn. She should be back soon. No way was there a line."

As if she was waiting for the perfect moment, Mia exits the bathroom with a slight look of disgust on her face as she wipes her hands down her skirt. Overdressed for the establishment, Mia looks smoking hot in an off the shoulder sweater that molds to her body like a glove and suede skirt.

"You survived!" Megan exclaims. "You deserve a drink for your bravery."

"On me," I add. "Both of you."

"Oh, I couldn't—" she begins to say, but Megan's "Hell yeah!" cuts her off.

"Brooksy, two vodka Red Bulls, please!" the blonde shouts over the jukebox.

Mia gives me an appreciative expression before Spencer steals her attention. "It's nice to officially meet you, Mia. I've heard a lot about you."

She glances at me, eyes wide, face stricken. She must suspect I saw the list and that I told Spencer about it. I would never, and only partially because he might want a shot helping.

"Not by this guy," my buddy states. "From Sunny." That must be who told him about the crash encounter earlier this week.

The pair launch into a discussion about where Mia is from in North Dakota, her life there, and Spencer's short-lived professional skiing career. While they talk, I take the time to watch, cataloging the way her eyes crinkle when she smiles and how she bites her lip to hold back from her grin spreading too wide.

Much too soon, Brooks delivers their drinks and the girls head off to a table to get "the full ladies' night experience," as Megan put it. My gaze travels back to them most of the night. I try not to be too obvious about it in front of Spencer and

Brooks, but I catch the latter staring at me knowingly. Bartenders have a sixth sense, I swear.

I've been waiting all night for an opportunity to get Mia alone, but it hasn't worked out. I almost resolve to try another day, but when Megan and one of the firefighters start to dance, my luck turns. Local creep, Benny Crowe, is chatting Mia's ear off, and if a damsel ever needed saving, it's this one. Time to shine.

10

Mia

THE FOUR BLISSFUL days of no contact from Steven came to an end this morning. Even though I blocked him, he somehow managed to text me from a different number. I assume he must have talked to my mom because he seems to know that I left town and that has him panicking.

His texts range from begging me to come home and astonishment that I actually left. None of them address the issues of our relationship and all have an undertone of "how can I do this to him?"

I thought I was keeping my emotions under wraps, but when Megan asked me what's wrong, I ended up spilling the beans about everything. Including my uncertainty if Jamies saw the list or not. As soon as we finished work for the day, Megan asserted that our plans for girls' night were that much more crucial and sent me on my way to get ready.

I've never been to Dirty Dick's, but she assures me it is casual. There weren't many places to go out in Trummings, and I find myself a little nervous to go into a new situation. That must be why I let Megan convince me to take two shots at her house before we head out the door.

Megan spent the first half of the night giving me all the gossip on the locals. She spent a little more time than she should on Spencer, specifically. I asked her if something was going on there, but she adamantly denied it. There's a story there I am determined to get eventually.

When a cute firefighter asks her to dance, she denies him at first. But I convince her I'll be fine on my own, and to enjoy herself. I didn't expect that the second she walked away, I would have company.

"Hey there, pretty lady. The name is Benny. I haven't seen you around before."

Taking in my new companion, I am not impressed. The vibe he gives off is this side of "I have candy in my van," and I am not interested. But ever the polite girl my mother raised me to be, I engage him in conversation nonetheless and hope I can make eye contact with Megan from across the room.

Right as one of Benny's clammy hands reaches out to touch my hair, a weight falls on my shoulder. Without having to glance up, I know it's Jamie.

"Hey, Benny. How are you?"

"James." He scowls at the younger man. "Can we help you?"

"Nah, I came over to join my girl since Megan seems to be otherwise occupied." Risking a glance, I see that Megan is no longer dancing, but arguing with Spencer, cute firefighter nowhere to be found.

"She didn't tell me she was taken," Benny mutters grumpily.

"Seeing as you two were simply talking, I wouldn't expect her to offer that information to a stranger," Jamie says, his voice feigning confusion. "You're welcome to stay and chat with us."

Benny declines the offer and returns to wherever he magically appeared from.

"Thanks for the save. He wasn't doing anything weird, but the vibe was off."

"Don't mention it. I've only been here a few months and it didn't take that long to hear about Benny, the local creep."

"For some reason, I assumed you were from around here," I admit. "You blend in with the Sugar Peak crew seamlessly. Where are you from originally?"

Jamie blows a raspberry, seemingly contemplating how to answer.

"I'm sorry if that is too forward," I rush out.

"It's not. It is just tough to answer. I've spent the last fifteen years working different jobs at resorts before taking this gig. I've worked in every province at various resorts, camps, and the like."

"What about growing up?"

"Kinda the same. My parents worked at resorts as well. We moved every couple of years."

"That's what you meant when you said they worked Christmas," I surmise, and he nods. "Is that why you hate it?"

"What does Jamie hate?" Megan asks, coming back with new drinks, Spencer trailing behind.

"Christmas," I reply.

"Dude!"

"How can anyone hate Christmas?" the newcomers say simultaneously.

"I don't hate Christmas," he clarifies. "I simply don't celebrate it to the degree other people do."

"What about Crosby?" I ask the question that's been weighing on my mind the past couple days.

"What about him?"

"Why would you name him after the King of Christmas if you aren't into the holiday?"

"The King of Christmas?" he echoes.

"Yeah, Bing Crosby."

"Oh, sweetie," Megan coos, passing me a drink as the guys stare at me in amusement.

"What?" I demand.

They share a glance before Jamie answers. "Crosby is named after Sidney Crosby."

"He's the center for the Penguins and, more importantly, was the last captain of the Canadian Olympic team when they won gold," Spencer adds, as if this is common information.

"Oh," I reply lamely. "I come from more of a football family."

"Don't worry about it, babe." Spencer laughs. He goes to pat my shoulder, but the arm Jamie still has slung over it blocks him.

"So you don't do anything Christmassy?" Megan asks, diverting attention from my blunder and back to the original issues.

"Not that I can think of."

"No Christmas movies? Caroling? Decorating? Baking cookies?" I question, each word coming out squeakier.

"Nope." He pops his p.

"What about hot chocolate?" Spencer asks.

"Hot cocoa is not a Christmas thing. It's a winter thing. I'm not a masochist. Of course, I enjoy cocoa. I'm never one to deny pleasure."

He speaks the last sentence while making direct eye contact with me, in a way that feels extremely intentional.

The four of us spend the next two hours talking and drinking before we call it a night. Since Megan lives in town, Jamie offers to drive me home to save her a trip. I was planning to stay in her spare room, but I'd much rather sleep in my bed, so I quickly agree.

The drive up the mountain is uneventful, mostly filled with Jamie telling me stories about the different places he worked. A few times, he reached over to give my leg a squeeze. I swear I can still feel the heat from that action radiating through my tights.

When we arrive back at the resort, he shuts off the engine and turns toward me. He must see the question on the tip of my tongue, because he answers it without prompting. "I always walk a lady to the door."

"For a grump, you are quite the gentleman," I tease.

"I'm not a grump," he challenges. "I'm a grinch."

Walking in the staff door, we both shake off our boots before venturing further in. Finishing before me, Jamie leans against the doorframe leading to the hallway, watching me. I expect him to move, but he remains firmly in place. When I reach him, his gaze flits up, and I see someone hung mistletoe.

My face immediately heats. "I didn't know that was there," I blurt out.

"I didn't think you did," he assures me. "But now that we're here... I'd really like to kiss you. In fact, I'm dying to kiss you. I haven't stopped wanting to kiss you since you landed on top of me in that lobby. Every time we're together, I can't help but crave your lips against mine."

I stare at him in disbelief. No one has ever craved me before. At least, no one who articulated it to me. I'm afraid a kiss from someone who craves me might ruin me. I'm also not sure I can say no. Before I get the chance to answer, he keeps going.

"The way I see it, you have three options. The first: you say no. I walk you to your door and we both pretend this never happened. The second: you say yes, and I kiss you the way a woman like you deserves to be kissed."

"How does a woman like me deserve to be kissed?" My voice sounds breathier than I've ever heard it, but if the goose-bumps shooting down my body are any indication, my body is fully on its own wavelength.

Jamie snakes an arm behind my back and pulls me into him. He uses his other hand to tuck a stray curl behind my ear and cup my jaw. "As if your lips carry the answers to all life's questions. As if without your kiss, I'd burst into flames of need and desire right where I stand."

A lump forms in my throat as I'm trapped in his gaze. Moments pass until I'm able to speak, and he waits patiently. "What's option three?"

A salacious grin takes over his features as he moves in. He runs his thumb over my cheek before kissing there and then my jaw. When his lips ghost my ear, I shiver in anticipation.

"Option three," he whispers, "is you let me kiss you like you deserve, and show you everything else you deserve. Allow me to help you check those items off your list. Let me help you discover what you want and give you pleasure beyond your wildest dreams."

The warm sensation in my stomach turns to lead, but before I can protest, he leans back so we're eye to eye.

"Don't panic," he cajoles. "There's nothing to be embarrassed about. We all have a list of things we want to do. You simply wrote yours down. With some rather clever names, I might add."

The hand on the back of my neck kneads softly, urging me to relax as he keeps going. "I'm drawn to you. I'm not ashamed to admit I feel a pull to you. You sense it, too. You have nothing to lose and everything to gain. I know you're still reeling from a breakup. We can keep it exclusive but casual. No one else has to know unless you want them to."

He's offering me the world on a silver platter. As much as I fantasized about trying new things, I would never be able to do it with someone I wasn't comfortable with, but I'm too raw to jump into something new right now. I trust Jamie. I have no doubt he knows what he's doing. It's a perfect proposition.

"What do you say, Mia?" he asks, staring at me hungrily. "Can I be on your naughty list?"

"Three," I all but whisper. "I choose option three."

Without giving me any time to second-guess myself, Jamie slams his lips into mine. Our bodies mold together as if we're one as he makes good on his word. Just as I feared, this kiss is ruining me. He's pouring his desire for me into it. I've never been kissed this way.

All too soon, he pulls back, leaving my lips tingling. Grabbing my hand, he walks me the rest of the way to my room. When he doesn't move to come in, I start to second-guess his willingness. Did the kiss change his mind?

He kissed the life out of me, but did he enjoy it? The way his mouth dominated mine, I didn't have any option but to follow along. Maybe I should have done more?

Before my thoughts can spiral out of control, he leans down and pushes a much more chaste kiss than we just shared against my lips. "As much as I would love to start now, you've had a lot to drink tonight and I don't want you to make any choices you'll regret. Text me when you're ready to talk and we can discuss everything with a clear head."

"Okay."

"Goodnight, Mia."

"Night."

When the door clicks behind me, I press my fingers to my still tingling lips and wonder what I just agreed to.

11

JAMIE

I SPENT the entire way walking back to my cabin wondering if I just made a grave mistake. Turning down Mia was one of the hardest things I think I've ever done. And that includes taking a bunch of tech bros who kept their eyes glued to their phones through a scenic hike in Banff.

It was so tempting to take her initial consent and run with it. But I don't wanna take advantage of her sweet nature, even though the way she was grinding against me while we kissed told me she was more than down.

Instead of dicking her down to within an inch of her life, I decided to be a gentleman and wait for her to come to me. And it's been a long day of waiting. So long that I've almost given up until a text comes through around three o'clock.

MIA

> Fancy coming to my place later for dinner and a movie?

> Absolutely. Have anything particular in mind? I can grab some food from the bar and bring it over.

> That would be great. I'm not picky. I'll be done working around six. I'm not sure what time you get off.

If things go as planned, hopefully I'll be getting off a couple of hours after six.

> As long as there's no emergencies, I should be off around that time. Meet you at your place at 7? Gives me some time to take Crosby home and feed him.

> See you then, Ebeneezer.

I arrive at Mia's door right on time. As soon as I knock, she ushers me into the sitting area where I saw the offending list the other night.

"I hope beer is okay," she states.

"Beer is great. It'll go perfect with the burgers."

As I set down our meals, she hovers nervously beside the couch and toys with the end of her sweater. Her nervous energy is palpable, and I wonder what I can do to set her at ease. I figure the best course of action is to take her literally and prepare to eat dinner and watch a movie.

"I wasn't sure what you wanted on your burger so I got everything on the side. You aren't allergic to dairy or gluten, are you?" I should've asked, but it slipped my mind.

Mia throws her head back and lets out a musical laugh, the

sound of which fills me with awe that I'm the one who made her make it. I don't even care that it was at my expense.

"I don't mean to laugh." She continues to giggle. "I was imagining the reaction my Nonna would have if one of her grandchildren couldn't eat pasta. I think she'd disown us."

"Fair enough," I reply. "I take it you're close with your family?"

"The town I'm from is small, and I'm pretty sure my family makes up about half of it. Didn't have much of a choice," she jokes.

"That sounds nice." I never wanted for more family, but it might have been nice to have some familial connection somewhere.

"What cinematic masterpiece do you have in store for me tonight?" I ask, wanting to keep the conversation on neutral ground. She still hasn't said if she wants to take me up on my offer, and as much as I'm dying to have her say yes, I don't want to pressure her.

When her eyes sparkle in mischief, I know I've made the right call. She clicks a few buttons on her remote and a green monster overtakes the screen. Alright, he may not be a monster. I'm not sure what the Grinch is, but he isn't human, that's for sure.

"Really?" I ask dryly.

"I want to get to know you better. I thought watching your biography would be a great way to do that," she says, settling down on the couch with her food.

"Hilarious."

We sit in companionable silence as we eat our food, commenting every so often on something on screen. When we both finish, she grabs our trash and tosses it in the bin. She sits back down beside me, stiff as a board, back to unraveling her sweater.

"Mia, listen," I start. "If I made you uncomfortable last night, I'm sorry. I didn't mean to invade your privacy, but I couldn't—"

She puts a hand up to stop my spiel. "It's not your fault. I'm the one who left the list out for the world to see."

"I don't know about the world, unless you were giving room tours after I left." She smiles at the joke.

"I'm sure you're wondering why I asked you here."

"You mean other than to give me nightmares of Jim Carey sneaking into my house?" Her shoulders loosen a fraction more.

"That's an added bonus," she replies. "Your proposition last night, did you mean it?"

"I did," I respond with no hesitation.

"You'd be willing to help me check some of the things off my list?"

"Hell yeah."

"Why?"

"Why what?"

She is biting her lip so hard, I'm afraid she's going to break the skin. Moving closer to her, I slowly raise my hand to her face so as not to startle her and pull her lip from her teeth, letting my thumb drag down her chin before resting it on her thigh.

She sucks in a deep breath before she answers. "Why do you want to help me mark things off my list? I mean, I know some of the things will benefit you, and I can certainly equal things out on the ones you don't get anything out of—"

"The hell I won't," I interrupt.

"What?" she asks, looking at me in confusion.

"Mia, I get 'something' out of everything on your list. I don't know what assholes you've been with before, but getting to touch you in any capacity is a privilege. Getting to come myself is icing on the cake."

"Asshol*e*," she murmurs.

"What?"

"Asshole. I've only been with one other person. We were together for ten years and—"

There's a sadness in her tone that really ticks me off at whoever this guy is. Not only did he hurt her, but he also made her think that her pleasure wasn't a priority. That ends today. Even if this is the only time I get to be with her, I want her to know that her pleasure matters.

"We don't need to talk about him. This list isn't about him. It's about you. What you like, what you want. And I want to be the one to help you discover that. Tell me I can. Tell me you'll let me show you what you've been missing out on."

Taking her jerky nod as consent, I slide the hand gripping her thigh back to her ass and pull her into me. When our lips meet, I thrust my tongue into her mouth. I don't want to give her time to second-guess her decision. I plan to overwhelm her with so much pleasure tonight, she lets me help her mark every single item off her list and maybe add a few more.

Her tongue brushes against mine deliciously, and my hands flex on her ass, pushing her down onto my leg to create a point of friction. When she moans into the kiss, I know I'm hitting the right spot.

After rocking her a few times, she gets the hint and takes over grinding against me, freeing my hands up to explore. As they move up her body, they lift her sweater with them. When I break her kiss so I can pull it all the way off, she whines.

"Don't worry, baby. I'm coming back." I laugh. A laugh that turns into a curse when I see her breasts in a lacy pink bra. "Fuck, Mia. These tits. Are they sensitive?"

Rubbing the pad of my thumb through the lace, a deep groan is my only answer. Duly noted. Wanting to explore further, I pull down the cups and suck one of her pink nipples into my mouth. I flick the other with my finger in time with my tongue.

"Jamie, holy shit," she whispers as her hands move to grip my shoulders. The heat of her center is so intense, I can feel it through my jeans. Now that she is fully relaxed, I think it's time to get working on the list.

She once again whimpers when I stop my ministrations.

"Mia, do you have a toy here?"

"What?" She blinks down at me.

"A dildo, vibrator, clit sucker. Do you have something like that here?"

"I— Why?"

"Because one of the entries on your list is to use a toy with a partner, right? We can order one if you don't, but I hope you have something you've been using to take care of what I know is a sweet pussy up until now."

"I have one," she whispers, blushing. I place a fast kiss on her lips to show she shouldn't be embarrassed.

"Go grab it. And lose the pants on your way back."

She scans my face hesitantly, as if she's searching for the joke, but she won't find one. I'd be happy to let her ride my face so we can check receiving oral off the list, though I do have questions about why it's on there. I'm hoping it's because she'd never come that way and not because her dickwad ex never tried.

Regardless, I figured a toy would be the easiest item to check off and help ease her into letting go with me. I also want to prove that I can get her off without reciprocation and be just fine.

She scurries off my lap and into the bathroom, giving me time to readjust my raging hard-on. As she walks back toward me, I get a perfect view of her tits bouncing since she got rid of the bra as well.

When she's slightly more than an arm's length away, she stops. In her hand, I spot a shiny pink vibrator. I turn my palm face up, silently asking her to drop it. The moment she does, I pull her back into my lap, this time facing outward. "Good girl."

She shivers at the praise, and I can't stop the grin that spreads across my face. It might rival the one the Grinch is making on screen. Speaking of, I hold her to me with one hand and turn off the TV with the other.

"Why'd you do that?" she asks.

"I can't have you looking at another man's face when you're coming for me. Now, let's see what this little guy can do."

I twist the end of the toy and the device comes to life. It's thin and only about four inches. Smaller than me, but it will do. "Do you have a favorite setting?"

"Um, I don't—"

Tsking, I slowly move the toy up and down her slit, coating it in the arousal she worked up grinding on me. "Don't lie to me, baby. This is about you and your fantasy. I want to make this good for you."

"It already is," she moans when I make a quick pass over her clit.

"Which setting?" I ask, nipping at her earlobe.

"Three," she breathes.

Turning the knob twice more, we get to a setting with a steady pulse. No patterns for this girl. We'll see about that. I don't want this to be a quick in and out. I want her to savor the experience.

I hold the toy lightly against her as I scoot forward to the end of the couch, allowing myself more leverage. "How's this?"

"Good," she answers, squirming for more pressure.

"There you go lying again, Mia. You gotta tell me what you

want. I'll make it happen, no matter what it is. If this is going to work, you have to communicate with me. Can you do that?"

"I'll try."

"That's all I ask." I reward her honesty by pressing the toy harder against her clit. It's then she lets out the same uninhibited moan she gave me last night when we kissed under the mistletoe.

"There it is," I coo. "Does this feel good? Do you like me using this cute toy to please you?"

"Yes," she murmurs, head leaning back into my shoulder.

"Are you pretending it's my tongue playing with your little clit instead? It's going to. You know that, right? I'm going to lick this pussy until I memorize the way that you taste."

When she bucks against the toy, I use the hand holding her to me to still her. "Not so fast, Mia. I control when you come, how you come. And I'm not done playing yet."

"I need more," she moans. "Please, Jamie."

"Such a good girl telling me what you need. I'll give you more."

I pull the toy away from her center and bring it to my lips. She watches me in rapt fascination as I lick the side.

"Fuck, you taste better than I imagined, sweet girl. Do you want a taste? Have you ever tasted yourself?"

She shakes her head and licks her lips. Taking that to mean she hasn't before but wants to now, I bring the toy towards her mouth. "Stick out your tongue."

My dick hardens more than I thought possible when she obeys. Head turned, she looks back at me, eyes shining with need, tongue waiting. When I tap the now off vibrator against it, she closes her lips around it and sucks. It takes Herculean strength not to toss her off me, pull out my dick and beg her to do that again with me in her mouth instead.

"That's it, baby. Make your toy nice and wet. I'm going to

slip it inside that needy cunt while my fingers rub against your clit. You want that, don't you? You want me to make you come with my fingers while you squeeze down on your vibrator."

I pull the toy from her mouth so she can answer. "Yes, please, Jamie. Make me come."

"Your wish is my command," I reply. She's soaked from my earlier attention. The vibrator slides right in. Once it is back on, I hold it with one hand while the other travels up to the apex of her thighs. I tap on her clit a few times before lightly circling it. The vibrations of the toy inside her causes tingles to erupt on my fingers.

As her breathing picks up, I sense her getting closer to her peak. "That's what you needed. You needed something to fill up that pretty pussy while I played with your clit. Are you going to come for me, Mia? Show me what a good girl you can be and give in to the pleasure."

It only takes a few more swipes of my fingers and she complies. I watched her fall apart beautifully in the reflection on the TV. Part of me regrets not getting a clear view, but if I have my way, this is the first of many times she comes for me.

I pull the vibrator out of her soaked core as I rub her through the aftershocks of her orgasm. I run my hand up and down her arm as her breath steadies, watching as goosebumps spread across her tan skin.

"You did so well," I murmur, pressing a kiss to her shoulder.

"Jamie, that was..." She trails off.

"I aim to please." I laugh, easing her onto her feet and off my lap. As much as I don't want to leave, I want to give her some time to process what happened, and we both have to work tomorrow.

When we're standing, she reaches for my belt, but I stop

her, grab her taunting, tiny robe, and drape it over her shoulders. "Not tonight."

"You don't want me to...?" she asks as she ties it closed. God, she's so cute. She just came sitting in my lap with a vibrator in her pussy, but asking if I want her to make me come makes her blush.

"Tonight was about you. We've got plenty on that list that will get me off, too. No need to rush it."

"Okay," she replies, yawning.

I try to stifle my grin, but I fail miserably, and she flushes further. "Sorry, I don't know why I'm so tired all of a sudden."

"I could wager a guess," I tease. Using the tie of the robe, I pull her in and press my lips to hers in a slow but passionate kiss.

"I'll text you in the morning. Sleep well."

"I will," she replies as she walks me to the door. My dick is just as hard on the walk back to my cabin as it was yesterday, but my mood is remarkably improved.

12

I FELL ASLEEP AS SOON as my head hit my pillow after Jamie left the other night. I've used that vibrator on myself an uncountable number of times and not once has it felt like that. Hell, thinking back to the handful of times in the last few years that Steven made me come, it never felt like that.

I don't know if it was the dirty talk or the intentionality of it all, but I know I'll never look at my vibrator the same again. I'm afraid I may have to buy a new one, as he ruined that one for me. Thank God he turned the movie off. I don't need that ruined for me as well.

Speaking of movies, I need to finish prepping the questions for the holiday movie trivia event I'm hosting later today.

As I'm scouring the web, my phone pings. Thinking it might be Jamie, I quickly pick it up. Unfortunately, it's not my hunky coworker. It's my can't-take-a-hint ex.

Of course he won't. Jeremy is the last single guy in his life. You'd have thought that was a sign he needed to think about settling down, but evidently not. The only other trip he goes on is with me to Trevor's, and there is no way he's going to be invited now that we're broken up. Tony was very clear on that.

If there is one thing I know about Steven, it's that he hates shopping; loathes it. There is no way he went to the mall during the busy holiday season to buy me an engagement ring. Either he's bluffing and planning to scramble and buy a ring later if this ploy works, or his mom went for him. Whatever way it happened, I'm not interested.

I was already over the relationship before Jamie made me come, but now? There is no way I could go back to being with someone who cares so little about if I get off or not. Maybe all men become that way eventually, but I don't remember a time he did more than make a feeble attempt at foreplay.

My experience the other night opened my eyes to a world

where someone puts in as much effort for you as you do them. And in that spirit, I am determined to help Jamie the same way he's helping me. Well, not the same way. I'm sure he's had no issues exploring things sexually. But I can help him find joy in the holidays. It can't be fun to see people around you so invested in the festivities while you feel nothing.

While writing trivia questions, I also start preparations for Operation Make Jamie Love Christmas. It's not the most inventive name, but it will do the trick. The list is simple.

Jamie's Holiday Hit List

- Kiss under the mistletoe
- Watch holiday movies
- Play in the snow
- Bake Christmas cookies
- Exchange presents
- Decorate a tree

We've checked two things off the list already. Though, I plan to force at least one more holiday movie on him. And I've heard several people mentioning we may be getting a snowstorm tonight, so the timing couldn't be better. The hardest one to accomplish is going to be getting him to decorate a tree, but I'm hoping I'll have some luck once we spend more time together.

"Alright, folks, this question is for the win. We'll be playing this Price is Right style: closest without going over. How much did Kevin McCallister spend on room service while staying at the Plaza?"

The sound of the bell has me turning to my right. "Greens, you rang first. What's your answer?"

"One thousand dollars," their ten-year-old son yells.

"Parkers, what's your answer?"

"One thousand and one!"

"Ballsy. I like it. Salvatores, your guess?"

Their teenage daughter grins at me, and I can already tell she's about to win. "$967.43."

"That's correct! Congratulations to the Salvatore family. You all win a free s'more setup any night during your stay. You can collect it at the cafe. Thank you to everyone who played. Don't forget to check out the other events we have happening during your stay, including a screening of *Four Christmases* in the theater."

Everyone makes their way out of the library where trivia was played, and I clean up the mess left behind. Once I'm done, I sink into one of the comfy chairs and congratulate myself for a job well done with a reread of my favorite romcom. If Piper can get the grumpy sea captain to appreciate the extra things in life, I can get my grinchy handyman to enjoy Christmas.

Well, not my handyman. Yikes. I need to keep that under control. He may have offered exclusivity, but who knows how long that will last once the list is complete. Though he did mention wanting to add to it. I'm not under any illusion he wants something permanent, but for now, casually exclusive is nice.

I must be more tired than I thought because some time between Brendan putting out the pan fire and Piper's trip to the hospital, I doze off. I wake to a gentle hand stroking my hair. When I rouse, I see Jamie crouched down in front of my chair.

"Hey, sleepyhead," he teases.

"Shoot. What time is it?"

"8:30 p.m."

"Thank goodness. I thought I slept here all night."

"Not this time, but I'll be sure to check the library on my morning rounds from now on to see if we have sleeping event planners. How was trivia?"

"Great! I was surprised how many people knew their stuff. What brings you here?"

"I was going to see if you wanted to grab dinner, but Lars broke the oven handle again, so I was delayed. When you didn't answer your door, I thought I'd better try here. Good thing I did."

Standing to his full height, Jamie offers a hand to help me up. Once I am, I gasp at the sight in front of me. The large windows at the other end of the library showcase the storm brewing outside.

"It's like being inside a snow globe," I whisper.

"Kind of is," he agrees from beside me.

"Come on," I say, dragging him out of the library and into the offices.

"What are we doing?" he asks, amused.

"You'll see!" Grabbing my coat, I take back his hand and head to the door leaving out to the deck.

13

JAMIE

IT DOESN'T TAKE LONG to realize Mia is taking us out into the snow. Since I don't live connected to the main lodge, I already have my heavy coat on. As Mia struggles into her parka, I can't help but think it's not going to keep her very warm, but she seems so excited, I don't want to stifle her joy. I can always warm her up after.

I'm grateful that Mia is cautious on the deck. I salted it earlier once we got word a storm was coming our way, but you can never be too careful. She bounds down the steps until she is back on solid ground, where she stands and twirls in a circle, trying to catch snow on her tongue. It reminds me of the way she stuck her tongue out for me and my cock stirs in my coveralls.

The thing that strikes me more than how sexy she looks is how free she seems. She's less inhibited, less conscious of what other people are thinking about her. It's a sight to see, and I'm the lucky bastard who gets to witness it.

Our encounter affected me more than I expected. Even though she didn't touch me, it feels as if she branded me somehow. I haven't been able to stop thinking about her since I met her, but now it's something more. Something I don't know if I've felt before. I am oddly invested in not just helping her complete her list, but her in general. I don't know what it means, but I'm interested to explore it further.

I'm rocked from my thoughts when something cold smacks against my face. Glancing up, I see Mia giggle as she packs another snowball. I try to move out of the way, but she nails me in the chest.

"Who taught you how to throw? A quarterback? Your aim is impeccable."

"I'll tell him you said so," she yells. Before I can question her, she whizzes a snowball past my head.

"You're in for it now, pretty girl. I hope you can run as well as you throw." I lunge toward her and she takes off. Unfortunately for her, my legs are longer and I have snow boots that were made for more than appearance. Catching her by the waist, I flip on my back, cushioning her fall as we hit the ground. The snow should be soft now, but I don't want to risk hurting her.

Peering up from the ground, I stare at her blinding smile as her chest heaves. Snow is falling all around us, quieting everything but our breathing.

"This position feels familiar," I tease. "You've got me. Now what are you going to do with me?"

"Depends, do you think what we've done classifies as 'playing in the snow?'"

"Hm, seeing as you got three shots in and I got none, I'd say you played, but I did not. Why?"

"Because it's on the list."

"I'm not sure this would count as semi-public play. For one, no one is anywhere near here. And for another, we're both fully clothed."

"Not my list, your list."

"My list?" I didn't realize I had a list, but if I did, fucking in the snow would not be on it. It's much too cold. "I don't think my dick wants to come out in the cold."

"It's not a sex list. It's a Christmas list."

"The only thing I want for Christmas is to feel your hot pussy wrapped around my cock. And maybe your mouth, if we have time."

"A Christmas *to-do* list," she huffs.

"And playing in the snow is on that list?"

"Yep. And it seems like we need more to check it off." With that declaration, she rolls off me and scoots out of reach. Before I can ask what she's doing, she flaps her arms and legs, making a snow angel.

"Make a snow angel, Jamie."

"When did you get so bossy?" I call over to her.

"This hot guy told me I had to start asking for what I wanted."

"Touché, sweet girl. Touché."

Conceding to her request, I quickly move my limbs enough to make a pattern in the snow and then jump up to view my handiwork. I'm not sure what the criteria is for snow angels, but it seems good enough to me.

Satisfied this can be marked off the list, I walk over to Mia and heft her over my shoulder.

"Hey!" she yells, pounding on my back. "What do you think you're doing?"

"I can hear your teeth chattering from over there. I'm taking your sweet ass back to my cabin, where I can warm you up and feed you. Crosby will be happy to have the company."

"Okay," she replies simply. Dropping her back on her feet, I grab her mitten-clad hand and guide her toward my truck. Once she slides inside, I lean over and buckle her in. It's a quick trip, but with fresh snow on the path, I want her secured.

When we arrive at my place, Crosby is elated to see her. The pooch barely gives me a second glance. I would be offended, but I don't blame him. I'd rather have Mia's attention, too.

Once we've gotten out of our outer layers, I point Mia to the couch. "Potato soup okay?"

"Sounds wonderful," she sighs. "You know, if you keep taking care of me like this, I'm going to get used to it and expect it from every man."

Peeking up from the can of soup I'm doctoring on the stove, I lock eyes with her. "Good. I hope you do." I also hope that man might be me, but I keep that part to myself.

14

Mia

While Jamie is in the kitchen making our soup, I watch him from my vantage point on the couch. When Crosby nuzzles my hand, I pet him absentmindedly. Is this what it's like to be taken care of? I gotta say, it's nice.

I don't know if my ex ever noticed or cared if I was cold or not. He certainly never made me soup to warm me up or make sure I was fed. I remember watching the way Zade doted on Molly during our Michigan trip last February. I thought it was because he was trying to win her over, but knowing him, he's probably like that all the time. I know Tony is with Rory. She may be a kick-ass boss babe, but she relishes when he coddles her.

But that can't be what's happening here, can it? This is a friendly thing. Or an I-want-to-have-sex-with-you-later-but-can't-if-you're-hypothermic thing.

When I stop petting him, Crosby makes a sound of discontent.

"My apologies, Mr. Wallace," I coo.

"Don't let him know he can boss you around or he'll never stop," Jamie says as he approaches with two steaming bowls of soup.

"Is the same true for his owner? Because I recall you getting a bit bossy the other night."

"Absolutely. He learned it from his daddy."

Shit. I know he didn't mean that sexually, but new kink unlocked.

"Naughty girl." He clicks his tongue, knowing exactly where my mind was. "Eat your soup before I have to spank you."

Fighting fire with fire, I reply back, "Yes, sir."

"Well played. Eat first, then I'll take care of your other appetite."

"What did you have in mind?"

He makes a locking motion in front of his lips. "Good girls wait." A cocky smirk crosses his features when I huff. "It will be worth it. I promise."

Grumbling, I concede. I've been trying to tamp down my horny since he tackled me earlier. You'd think the cold would calm my libido, but it did nothing to quell my need.

"Oh my God," I moan after my first spoonful. "This came from a can?"

"The base did," he replies. "But I zhuzhed it up with a few things I had in the kitchen."

"Compliments to the chef," I say. This soup is doing wonders to warm me from the inside out. I do a little dance as it hits my taste buds. When I finish, Jamie takes the bowl from me and deposits it in the sink along with his own.

"Come on," he prods.

"Where are we going?"

"To finish warming up. How do you feel about checking two things off your list tonight?"

"Which two?" I ask as he leads me into a decent sized bathroom for the small cabin. He reaches in the shower stall to turn on the water. "Shower sex?"

"Mhmm."

"What's number two?" I question nervously.

"Do you trust me?" His question takes me aback. I've only known him for a week, but I realize that I do trust him. If I didn't, I wouldn't be isolated in this cabin with him.

"Yes."

Jamie brushes his thumbs along my cheeks in a way that tells me he's pleased with my answer. "Good. Number two is a surprise."

Before I can protest, he drops to his knees. My breath hitches as he slowly unbuttons my jeans and tugs them down my legs, panties with them. When they catch on my socks, he lifts one foot and then the other to remove them. Once my bottom half is bare, he kisses slowly up it before pressing a soft kiss to my mound. I wonder if oral is going to be the next thing checked off, but he rises, removing the hockey sweater I wore for trivia as he does.

Once the garment is removed, his lips graze my neck. "I didn't realize you were a Blackhawks fan."

"I'm not. Clark wears one in *Christmas Vacation*. It's pretty iconic."

"Haven't seen it." I'm momentarily distracted by his reply as he nips the delicate skin behind my ear.

"I'll add it to the list. You have too many clothes on."

He takes a step back, and I instantly miss the heat his body took with it. Staring into my eyes, he makes quick work of removing his clothes so he's as naked as I am. When he's done, I can't help but gawk.

Jamie is ripped. I knew he was in great shape, but I did not expect the muscle definition or the Adonis belt. As my eyes travel down his body, my thighs instinctively clench when I get to his cock. Seeing as I only have one to compare it to, I don't know if I'd say it's massive, but it is definitely larger than what I've dealt with before.

My gaze shoots back up to his cocky smirk. "Don't worry. I'll make sure your pussy is nice and wet so you can take it all."

I want to protest that there is no way that thing is going to fit, but I'm cut off by him pushing me into the shower. I let out a content sigh as the warm spray washes over me.

"This is nice," I say when I sense him behind me.

"It's about to get a lot nicer."

I hear the snap of a bottle behind me, and for some reason, my brain goes straight to lube. He must have brought lube to make sure I'm wet enough for him.

I jerk when his fingers touch my scalp. "What are you doing?" I sputter.

"Washing your hair," he replies, bemused. "Do you not want it washed?"

"Yes. No. I mean, I can do it."

"So can I. Turn around."

"You're being bossy," I grouse, obeying.

"I think you like it when I'm bossy," he muses. I melt as his deft fingers work the shampoo into my hair and the shower fills with the smell of eucalyptus. It's not the scent I would have chosen for him, but it's nice.

"You're so good at this," I compliment.

"Thank you. I've been washing my own hair for thirty years now," he teases.

"You know what I mean."

He laughs. "I do. It comes naturally with you, it seems. Taking care of you is intrinsic. Plus, your body tells me exactly what you like most."

Washing out the shampoo, he repeats the process with conditioner until I'm a puddle in his hands. When he suds up his hands to wash my body, my senses come back online. Similar to the other night, Jamie is positioned behind me.

He starts slowly, massaging my shoulders, down my arms and over my ass. He kneads slowly as he travels up my stomach. When he gets to my breasts, he cups them in his hands.

"You have the most amazing tits I've ever seen," he whispers into my ear. "They're fucking perfect."

Inspired by his words, I push my ass into him and grind against him as he tweaks my nipples into hard peaks.

"I think my breasts are clean," I whine as my knees start to feel like Jell-O.

"You think so? Is there somewhere else I should focus my attention?"

"Jamie," I plead, not knowing exactly what I'm asking for, but knowing I need something. Thankfully, he doesn't make me verbalize my desires and moves his hands back down my torso until they reach the space between my legs.

"Can I tell you a secret? When I was fucking you with your vibrator the other night, I was jealous I wasn't able to feel this sweet pussy clench around my fingers. Let's rectify that now, yeah?"

"Yes, please."

"I love when you beg for me," he groans. "Fuck, you're wet, Mia."

Jamie smoothly plunges two fingers into my heat. "Oh my God."

"You're so tight. I'm going to have to stretch this pussy out so it can take my dick." I'm not sure if he's saying that for my benefit or simply talking out loud, but he begins to do just that. I expect him to add another finger, but instead he begins to scissor the ones inside me. When he hits a spot in me that forces me to slam my hands against the wall, he stops.

"Was that the spot, baby? Is that where you need me to rub so you'll come for me?" He grazes it again, and I moan.

"Yes, yes. Right there." Heeding my request, he focuses his attention on massaging that spot, passing it over and over as he scissors his fingers inside me. His other hand moves up, collaring my throat so that I can't move away from him. Not that I'd try.

I'd be more likely to drown in this shower than pull away from him right now. The coil of need in my lower belly is wound so tight, I'm afraid I'll burst into flames when it breaks. Jamie's hands are the only thing tethering me here.

"That's it. I can feel that pussy fluttering against my fingers," he coos as he adds a third. "So full, aren't you, baby? You're going to love how stuffed you'll be with my fat cock inside you. You want to feel full of me and come with me inside you, don't you?"

I garble what I hope sounds like a yes, because I want that very much.

"Come on my fingers first. Soak my hand, so I know this pussy is nice and wet for me." As he continues to whisper dirty things in my ear, he hones back in on that spot I love so much. Just when I'm afraid I'm going to teeter on this edge forever, he leans down and bites into my shoulder. The added sensation is just what I need to shatter in his arms.

The moment I come down from my orgasm, he spins me around to face him. He captures my lips in a searing kiss that pours his desire into me. I grip his shoulder to gain leverage as he ravages my mouth, allowing him to grab my thighs and lift me in the air. I instinctively wrap my legs around him, nestling his cock between my folds.

Glancing down, I see he's already sheathed himself in a condom. "You did so well. You earned yourself a two-for-one special," he cajoles.

"Is that two orgasms?" I pant.

He tips his head back in laughter. "Technically, you will be getting two orgasms, yes. But no, it's two things from your list. Shower *wall* sex. Think you can handle it?"

"Are you sure you can hold me up that long?" I ask hesitantly.

Wall sex is always something I wanted to try. It seemed so romantic and passionate. The one time we tried it, Steven complained that it was too hard to get leverage while also supporting my weight. I'm an average sized girl. You'd think a wrestling coach would have had more upper body strength.

"Don't worry about me. The only thing you need to worry about is taking this dick like a good girl and coming so hard you pull me over the edge with me."

"You have such a dirty mouth."

"I think you'll find my mouth is good at a lot of things, pretty girl," he replies. "Are you ready?"

"Fuck me, Jamie."

Not needing to be told twice, Jamie lines his cock up with my entrance. I expect him to inch in, but he seats himself in one firm thrust, causing me to cry out at the intrusion.

"You okay?" He stills, allowing me to adjust to the feeling and size of him inside me.

"So big." He wasn't kidding when he said I'd feel full. I don't think I've ever felt so full before, but I revel in it. I revel in the way he fills me up. The way his jaw ticks, as if he's trying to hold off from enjoying himself too much. The way he watches where he plunges into me with rapt attention as he starts to move.

I feel weightless when I'm with Jamie. And not because he's literally holding me up right now. I feel weightless against expectations: mine, my family's, the world's. He doesn't seem to want anything but my true, authentic self—and orgasms.

Touching my body, feeling me come on his fingers is what triggers the wildness in his eyes, and that's heady. Wanting him to feel as good as I do, I lean forward and pepper his neck with kisses. His cock jerks inside me as he picks up his pace.

"I knew this pussy would be perfect," he groans. "It was made for me. I don't think I will ever be able to leave it again."

"Don't," I mewl as he pushes into me over and over. "You feel so good inside of me."

The shower has to be lukewarm at this point, but my skin is boiling. Heat is radiating through my body, and he continues to pound into me. The grip he has on my thighs is so tight, I know there will be bruises tomorrow, but I don't care.

Never in my life have I felt this wanton, this out of control. I'm impressed by the control Jamie seems to still possess as his thrusts grow harder but no more frantic. "I want to feel you come inside me," I moan.

"You will," he replies, pausing to circle his hips. "You've got to come for me again first, though. Two-for-one, remember?"

"I don't know if I can. I've never come twice before," I confess.

"Good. We can add it to the list and cross it off, then. We'll call it *Miracle on 34th Street*."

"That doesn't make any sense." I laugh between moans.

"Sorry, my blood flow is currently somewhere other than my brain. We'll pick a better name later. After I make you do it. Now, be a good girl and come on my dick so I can feel this pussy clamp down on me."

With a renewed sense of purpose, he tilts my hips and pounds into me. This new angle has him not only hitting the spot he found earlier, but also dragging against another I didn't know existed.

"Jamie, Jamie," I chant his name as I hurtle quickly toward my climax. The wave overtakes me faster than expected and I cry out as I come for him. As if my orgasm sets off his own or he was holding back for me, he follows right behind, resting his head on my shoulder as he empties into the condom inside me.

As we—he—stand there catching our breaths, I feel everything; parts of my body I didn't know I could feel, I'm feeling. Whatever just happened in this shower rebooted my entire system.

"That was incredible," he pants, lifting his head and kissing my lips softly. I immediately miss him when he pulls out. When he gets back from disposing of the condom, he must read my expression because he boops my nose and tips my face up to his.

"Don't worry, baby. I'll be back inside you again soon. But first, let's get you clean again."

Once we're sufficiently clean, he pulls a soft t-shirt over my head after drying me with a fluffy towel. I crawl into his bed as he lets Crosby out one last time. When he comes back in, I take my time enjoying the view of him stripping back down to only his boxers.

As he crawls beside me, wrapping me in his arms, contentment washes over me. I fall asleep quickly to the sound of the wind whipping the snow outside and the calming sensation of Jamie drawing circles on my thighs.

15

Mia

I wake up the same way I fell asleep, wrapped up in Jamie's arms. I'm surprised how much I enjoy the position. Even when we first started spending the night together, Steven and I didn't sleep cuddled up together. It's nice.

Just when I think he's asleep, a cool hand sneaks its way under the hem of the shirt I slept in, causing me to squeak. "Cold!"

"Sorry," he chuckles. "Crosby insists I accompany him when he goes out in the mornings. I didn't wear gloves, hoping it would be quick. He was not as concerned about time as I was. I didn't wake you up, did I?"

"Nope. I'm surprised. I'm usually a light sleeper."

"Hmm, must have been worn out," he muses against my ear, nuzzling into me. "So warm."

"What time is it?"

"It's around seven, why?"

"Today is my first staff meeting. There's going to be an exciting announcement."

"Oh, yeah? What's that?"

"I can't tell you," I reply.

Not happy with my answer, Jamie rolls us until he's looming over me. "Tell me."

"No way! I've been sworn to secrecy. Besides, it's Christmas related, so I'm sure you won't be interested anyway," I tease.

"If you're involved, I'm interested."

A thrill shoots through me, both at the words and the heat in his gaze. I bite my lip and shake my head in a show of defiance. There is an announcement, but I doubt it's a secret, and even if it was, I doubt he would tell anyone in the three hours before it's revealed.

"I have ways I can get you to talk," he whispers against my lips, kissing me firmly.

"I'm a vault."

"We'll see about that, baby."

I gasp when he grinds his pelvis against mine. He uses the opportunity to slide his tongue into my mouth and deepen the kiss. Too soon, he pulls away and lifts his weight off of me. Before I can protest, he slides down, head escaping under the covers.

"What are you doing?" I question.

"You know what I'm doing," he replies.

It isn't until he softly bites my thigh that it registers. "You don't have to—"

My protest is silenced by another bite. His callused hands grasp the backs of my legs, pushing them wider apart so that he can wedge his broad shoulders in.

I expect him to dive right in, but he doesn't. He slowly licks up one side until he reaches the apex and down the other, avoiding all my most sensitive spots.

His arms have my hips pinned down so I can't seek any friction. Frustrated at his teasing, I whine. "Jamie, please."

That does the trick, and he shifts his attention where I want him. He flattens his tongue and presses it firmly against my clit. I shudder at the foreign sensation. When he begins to flick, I swear my soul leaves my body. The noise I let out is inhuman.

Is this what I've been missing out on all these years? If so, I'm pissed. This is amazing. I never want it to end. Through the way heat is building in my core, I'm afraid it will, too soon.

I move my hands into his hair but bring them away quickly.

"Pull my hair. You won't hurt me," he huskily commands. Heeding it, I return my hands to his short blond strands and grip. If I can't grind against him, at least I can do this.

As I expected, I am hurdling to an orgasm quicker than anticipated when he switches from flicking my clit to sucking on it. Wanting to see him, I rip the sheet off us and find his eyes staring back at me.

When my breath catches at the sight, I feel him grin against me. "Feel good?"

"Yes, yes. It feels amazing. I'm so close," I moan.

"Good. I want you to come for me," he coaxes. "I want you to come while my face is between your legs. Then, I'm going to flip us so you can ride my face while you suck my cock."

God, I want that. I want to grind against his mouth as he fills mine. Taste him the way he's tasting me. The way my fingers tighten on his hair must tell him as much. He doubles his efforts to send me over the edge. He licks and sucks and flicks my clit relentlessly. When his teeth graze against it, I explode, shouting his name.

He slowly guides me through the end of my release before placing soft kisses on my thighs. I expect him to crawl up and kiss me. Instead, he makes good on his earlier promise. Keeping hold of my hips, he thrusts his weight to the side until he's on his back and I'm looking down at him. As I hover above him, I can't help but notice the wetness across his mouth and chin. My wetness. I may have just come, but the sight of him coated in my arousal has me ready for round two.

"Turn around, baby. It's time for riding lessons, part one. Let me show you what it's like to be with a two-seater."

And show me he does. I finish a second time before he rolls us once more and fucks me into the mattress. When he walks me back to my room so I can get ready for work, both of us forgetting the secret he wanted to know, I check two more items off my list.

16

JAMIE

SCANNING THE FULL LIBRARY, I search for a seat for our team meeting. Spencer catches my attention and nods to the spot beside him.

"Thanks, man," I reply when I plop down next to him. Before I can strike up further conversation, our de facto manager opens the meeting.

"Good morning, everyone," Hadley says. "Thank you, everyone, for meeting today, especially those of you who are technically off the clock. I'll try not to take up too much of your time. With two weeks until Christmas, I wanted to ensure we were on the same page."

Hadley continues to speak, but my mind is elsewhere as I search the room for Mia. It doesn't take long to find her standing near the front of the room. As if she can sense my gaze upon her, her eyes peer up from the paper she is reading and meet mine. A pretty blush crosses her features, causing her to bite her lip and turn her attention back to the front of the room.

"Man, you've got it bad," Spencer comments beside me.

"Fuck off," I mumble quietly, as to not catch the attention of the other staff around us.

"I'm not saying it's a bad thing. A relationship looks good on you."

"I don't know if I will call what we have a relationship. She just got out of something serious and I've never really done that before."

"Call it what you want," he scoffs. "But the way the pair of you are mooning across the room at each other is pretty damn obvious."

"She's mooning at me?" I ask. I know I was mooning at her, but to think she was matching my energy makes a man feel good.

"You're ridiculous, bro. Just admit—"

"Shh, Mia's talking now," I chastise, noticing her up at the front.

I can't help from watching the way she moves as she speaks to the crowd. The velvet dress she's wearing perfectly hugs all of her curves without putting her on display. All I can think about is pulling on the tie that holds it around her and unwrapping her like a present. Now that's the kind of Christmas gift I can get behind.

Speaking of Christmas gifts, I hear the term come out of her mouth and redirect my attention to what she is saying.

"In order to show his appreciation for the staff, Mr. Oliveira has graciously offered to host a staff Christmas party. The party will take place on the twenty-third and will include Secret Santa. Make sure you come up to the front of the room before you leave so you can pull the name of your giftee.

"And before any of you ask, the catering is going to be done by local businesses in Sugar Peak, so there will be no added work on your part to put this event together."

I hate giving gifts. Nine times out of ten, people don't want what you get them, and you wasted your time and money. I wonder if I can bribe my way into getting Spencer or Mia as my giftee. I at least know what they enjoy.

"Thank you, Mia, for the rundown of all the events we have the rest of this holiday season, and for the news of our Christmas party. Are there any other announcements? Maintenance?"

"Just a quick reminder for everyone that after the snow we had last night, some of the cabins on top of the mountain are going to need repairs before our next set of guests arrive. If there are any last-minute bookings, please let me know so I can prioritize those first."

"Thank you for that, Jamie. If there is nothing else, I will let everyone get back to their day. I'll be sending out an email recapping this meeting for those who could not join."

Standing from my seat, I hang back with Spence as people scurry to go pull their name.

"You're off today, right?" he questions.

"Yeah, though I'm sure I'll find something to fix."

"You wanna meet me up top to snowboard?" It's been a while since I've taken advantage of the biggest perk of working at Sugar Peak: all the free skiing and snowboarding I can handle. Between unforeseen maintenance issues and spending my spare time with Mia, it's been a while since I've hit the slopes.

"Sounds good. I need to eat first, though."

Spencer and I part ways after agreeing to meet at the mountaintop bar for pizza. We'll hit some of the lesser known trails after that. After this morning, I am hoping I'll get to end my day the way I started it, between Mia's legs.

With only a few stragglers left in the library, I head to where she stands at the front.

"Was this your big secret, Miss Ricci?"

"Maybe." She shrugs. "It was an easy way to force you to check off exchanging gifts from your Christmas bucket list."

"About that. Am I ever going to get to see this list or is it just something you've made up in your head that you can add to at your whimsy?"

"Are you suggesting I don't take list-making seriously, Mr. Geller?" she sasses back. The urge to grab her ponytail and pull her into me for it is strong, but we aren't alone and I don't think she'd be up for that kind of PDA. Exhibitionism is not on her list.

"I would never make such an accusation. I'm here to find out what unlucky soul is getting a gift from me. And to ask what you're doing later this afternoon."

"If you had been paying any attention in the meeting earlier, you would've known that we have our gingerbread house competition at three. And then I have plans to test out a new treat that I'm hoping to offer at the Boxing Day event. You clearly were not listening."

"My apologies. I was too busy remembering what it felt like when you came against my lips this morning. And wondering how those boots would feel against my back when your thighs are wrapped around my face."

Her bravado falters as her face and chest flush a pretty crimson. She smacks my chest when I chuckle at her reaction.

"I'll see you later," she huffs, pretending to be annoyed.

"I look forward to it. Let me know if you need any help taste testing."

17

JAMIE

AFTER A GREAT AFTERNOON shredding the trail with Spencer, I head to my cabin to shower and feed Crosby his dinner. Once we've both eaten, I decide to see what Mia is up to. When she asks if she can come over to make cookies since she doesn't have an oven in her room, I quickly agree. Cookies and the potential for hot sex? Count me in.

"Did you preheat the oven?" she asks as I usher her in.

"I did. And don't think I don't know this is a ploy to get me to do Christmassy things."

"You caught me," she snickers. "But I did find a dog-shaped cookie cutter, so we can decorate a gingerbread Crosby along with Mia and Jamie. He can't eat his cookie self, though."

"He'll get over it. Although, I don't know how I feel about eating the cookie version of myself. I can think of other cookies I'd much rather eat."

99

"That was cheesy," she replies, unpacking her supplies on the small island in the middle of my kitchen. "You clearly spent too much time with Spencer today."

"He does tend to rub off on me. And not the fun way."

"Jamie! You're incorrigible."

She moves to swat my chest, but I catch her hand and use it as leverage to pull her against me. She protests at first, but melts into me as I bring our mouths together. Once I kiss the argument off her lips, I release her, letting her get back to the task at hand.

I start to ask how I can assist when Crosby pops his head in between us, demanding attention. Mia complies and pets the pup, who nuzzles into her, soaking up the affection I was hoping to receive, side-eyeing me the entire time.

"Okay, I need to get to work if these are going to have time to cool," she says, ending her pats. With a disgruntled sigh, Crosby trots over to the door, where he sits and glares at me.

"I think he's trying to tell you something," she giggles.

"I told you he'd get bossy."

"Must get it from his daddy," she quips.

"Careful, baby," I tsk. "Don't start something you can't finish. I'd hate for your cookies to burn because you were too busy screaming my name."

She takes a moment to consider my proposition, but we're interrupted by a canine groan.

"To be continued," I say, giving her a quick kiss.

My snow-loving dog decides to take his sweet time outside. By the time I get back home, Mia is popping the cookies into the oven. When she turns around, my heart climbs into my throat.

She's standing in my kitchen with her thick hair up in a messy pile, with flour marks on her cheeks, and in nothing but an apron.

"Holy shit," I mutter, thankful that my cabin is small and it only takes me a few strides to reach her. "You're a wet dream, baby."

"Oh, yeah?"

"Yeah. If Lars looked half as sexy as you do, maybe people would be more inclined to put up with his shitty attitude. Hot baker is working for you."

The giggle that leaves her has my heart soaring and my cock stirring. I never knew you could experience both at once, but this girl is living proof.

Picking her up, I sit her down on the only clean sliver of counter I can see and move myself in between her legs. As she hisses at the cold sensation on her ass, I bring my lips to her neck, where I suck tiny marks. Nothing long enough that they will be visible tomorrow, but with enough suction to have her arching into me.

Over her shoulder, I spot a bowl of green goo that I realize must be icing. Reaching out, I move it closer and I stick my finger inside. Bringing it to my lips, I smile when the sweet taste hits my tongue.

"That's for later," she warns.

"Trust me, you'll much prefer how I use it right now." Dipping my finger back into the mixture, I brush icing onto her bottom lip, smiling when she licks it up.

"Want more?" She nods enthusiastically, and I move my finger back to her mouth.

"Suck," I command. My cock hardens to steel in my sweats as she does. I desperately want to pull it out and fuck her on this counter, but first, we have an item to check off the list: food play.

My hand moves to the top of the apron where it loosens the tie, allowing me access to her perfect breasts. So perfect that I can't stop myself from telling her that.

"I always thought I was an ass man, but these tits. I would build a shrine to them, baby." She attempts to pull her thighs together at my admission, seeking friction, but my body blocks her.

Swiping another dollop of icing, I paint it across her nipple. Leaning down, I softly lick the pebbled bud. "So sweet."

"Jamie," she moans when I give it a proper suck, tongue circling it inside my mouth. The combination of the icing and her natural taste drives me wild. I'd planned to draw all over her body in the sticky substance, but the way her nails are biting into my shoulders tells me she can't wait that long either.

Shifting my attention to the other nipple, I offer it a similar treatment. I tug it lightly with my teeth as she writhes under me, body caged in my own.

"Fuck me, Jamie. Please."

"So needy tonight, baby. You clearly had a plan standing in my kitchen in nothing but an apron. Is that what you wanted? Me to fuck you up on this counter?"

"No," she replies hoarsely.

Confused, I pull back. "No?"

"No. I wanted you to bend me over and fuck me from behind." Shit. Her request has my cock so stiff, it's slipping out my waistband.

"You're getting so good at asking for what you want. That's what you want, Mia? You want me to press your pretty tits into the cold metal and slam into this perfect cunt until it clamps down on me?"

"Yes, please, Jamie. Take me hard."

With a final hard kiss to her lips, I pull her down and press her against the metal island. She hisses at the mix of sensations, body hot for me but metal cold. I consider using the apron strings to tie her up, but we're flying through her list and I'm not ready to face what happens once we get to the end. I'll find another opportunity to tie her down and maybe tie her to me more permanently.

Pushing my sweats down to my knees, I quickly sheath myself before tilting her hips to the perfect height. She's braced on her tiptoes, meaning she has no leverage and will be forced to take what I give her. And I plan to give her everything. Fuck her so hard she can't think of anything but my cock filling her up.

"Ready?"

"Yes, please," she begs. "Fuck me."

I rub the head of my cock between her lips, coating myself in her arousal. She mewls when it clips her sensitive nub. I'd love to spend more time teasing it, but I'm afraid I'll combust if I don't get inside her soon.

Moving back slightly, I watch as my cock thrusts into her in one smooth stroke. Her hand slams on the counter, looking for purchase, but there isn't any. Unlike the last time we fucked, I don't give her time to adjust. I pull out of her to push back in harder.

I set a punishing pace. My need for her is too great to go slow or be gentle. I'll make it up to her after by licking her pussy until she passes out. For now, we're both too crazed for anything but this.

Her knuckles turn white as her fingertips scrape the counter. "Jamie, so good. Don't stop," she cries. As if I was capable of stopping. I'm already holding myself back from blowing as I try to push her over the edge first.

Removing one hand from her hip, I reach between her legs and stroke her soaked core. Finding her clit, I rub quick circles.

"Mia, I need you to come for me. I can't last much longer in your hot pussy. You're gripping me so tight. You need to come on my cock." I sense the moment she reaches the peak as her body tenses below me.

She chants my name as she shatters on my cock, bringing me over the edge with her. Heat shoots down my spine as my balls tighten, my release rocking through me.

Every time I'm with her, I swear it's the best. And then the next time happens. I don't know how she manages, but I'm not one to question good fortune. And getting to be with Mia is the best fortune I've ever had.

Once we catch our breaths, I send her off to shower while I take out the cookies and heat up what was left of my dinner so she can have some real food.

<hr>

"This stir-fry is amazing," she moans, spearing a piece of chicken and a carrot into her mouth.

"I'm glad you think so. And I'm even more glad you're eating more than just cookies today."

"The cookies would have been better if they'd had more icing," she grumbles half-heartedly. "Besides, according to Buddy, there are only four food groups: candy canes, candy, candy corn, and syrup."

"Yeah, well, the grown man elf isn't exactly a role model in nutrition. And I'm partial to our use of icing. We can always try again in the morning with maple syrup."

She does the most adorable shoulder shimmy as she finishes her simple meal and considers my suggestion. "We may need to push that back. My pussy needs a break after tonight, and this morning, and last night..."

"Shit, was I too rough with you?" I didn't consider the fact that we'd already had sex twice in the last twenty-four hours. She's gotta be sore.

"I'm fine," she replies, waving off my concern. My eyes

roam her as if I can spot any damage as we're bundled up on the couch. "I swear," she reiterates as she catches my perusal. "My pussy isn't used to this much action. My ex and I only had sex a few times a month."

The ex. Part of me wants to kick his ass for clearly treating her poorly. Another wants to shake his hand because it landed her here with me.

"You said you guys were together for a while?" I attempt to fish casually. I don't want to bring up bad memories, but now I'm desperate to know where they stand. Am I simply a rebound for her? That's what I was hoping for at first, but now, I want more.

I've never enjoyed someone's company the way I enjoy hers. And not strictly the sexy moments, but the domestic ones as well. If you'd told me I'd have fun decorating Christmas cookies or cleaning my kitchen, I would have questioned your sanity. But now, I can see it. I've lived in a lot of places, but nowhere has felt as much like home as this cabin has in the last couple of weeks. And I know she's a big part of that.

The more time I spend with her, the more I realize I'm willing to do a hell of a lot of things—including enjoying Christmas—if it means I get to keep her.

"About ten years," she replies. "He was friends with my brother in high school, but I was several years younger so he never spared me a second glance. We started dating when he moved back after college. I was so excited he'd finally given me the time of day, I missed the red flags. By the time I saw them, we were already in too deep. Our friend groups were merged, my parents loved him, it made sense to keep the status quo."

"What happened that had you fleeing to another country to get away from him? Did he hurt you?" The idea that he may have sets my blood on fire. I haven't used my passport in years, but I'm willing to fish it out and fly to her hometown to kick his ass if I have to.

"No, nothing like that," she assures me. "Actually, nothing happened. And that was the problem. Ten years dating, several living together, and we were in this routine we couldn't get out of. I guess more accurately, he didn't want us to get out of.

"All our friends were getting married and having kids, but there was always one more thing he wanted us to accomplish before we could take that step. And they weren't even cool things, like travel or winning gold medals. They were dull, achievable goals."

"You haven't traveled much, then?"

"I can count the number of flights I've taken in my life on two hands," she sighs. "This is probably the farthest I've ever been from home. It's certainly the longest. I'd like to travel more, though."

"You should. The offseason is a few months, plenty of time to explore somewhere new and come back. If you plan to come back, that is."

"Yeah," she replies, lost in thought. I want to push her for more, but not ready to put my own cards on the table, I hold back. There's one more question I need to ask.

"Do you still love him?"

"No," she answers quickly. "I don't know if I have for a while. It was just easy to stay the course, ya know? Untangling our lives would have been difficult. Maybe that's why I saw running away as the best solution."

Her reasoning makes sense, even if I see a flash of something—regret, shame, sadness?—in her eyes. It's gone before I can be sure. Not wanting to dampen the mood further, I tug her closer until she is practically on my lap and turn my attention back to the movie.

"I wish I had Spencer as my Secret Santa," I state.

"Why's that?"

"I think he'd look hot in some Christmas lingerie like Buddy got his dad, don't you think?"

She breaks out in a fit of giggles that I can't help but join her in. Mood lightened, I settle in, relishing the way she rests her head on my chest. We have months to figure out this thing between us. No use stressing out about every last detail now.

18

Mia

Jamie's question about my future plans plague me the next two days. When I accepted the job from Hadley, it was through the end of the season, and to be honest, I hadn't thought further ahead than that. I was entirely focused on getting out. I didn't think further than the next few months.

Hopefully, the resort will agree to keep me on. I don't know what I would do otherwise. I really enjoy the work we've done here and have so many ideas for events we can host moving forward, even in the offseason. I know going back home is not an option. I'm not ready to face my family's scrutiny and I've felt more myself these past few weeks than I have in years.

As if she can sense my thoughts, my phone buzzes beside me with a call from my mother. I know if I don't pick up, she'll continue to blow up my phone, so I swipe the answer button and put her on speaker. If I have to talk to her, at least I can multitask and wrap my Christmas present for the holiday party.

"Hi, Mom."

"Look who finally deigned herself good enough to talk to her mother."

"We texted three days ago," I deadpan.

"Texting is not a phone call. I can't tell how you are over a text. There's no inflection or tone of voice. I need to know if my baby is okay."

That's sweeter than I would have expected from her. It's not that my mom is a bad mother by any means. She took care of Tony and I our entire lives. She simply has different values and ideas of what my life should be.

"I certainly can't tell if you're lying or not." And there it is.

"Why would I lie to you, Mom?"

"I didn't think that you would, but I also didn't think you'd be harboring a secret plan to run away to God knows where."

"Several people know where I am," I correct.

"But not your own mother! I didn't realize you could be so irresponsible. What will they do if you have some sort of accident and they need to contact your next of kin?"

"I listed Tony as my emergency contact and medical power of attorney." I need to make a note to remind Tony that Mom doesn't know the name of the resort. I have no doubt she'll try to weasel it out of him. He may be smart, but he can be gullible.

"Your brother? Over your own mother?" she gasps.

"He is a doctor, Mom. Isn't he your medical decision maker, too?"

"Well, yes, but that's because I don't want to put your father in the uncomfortable position of trying to grieve whatever has happened to me and make complex medical decisions."

"Got it," I say, setting down the scissors I was using to cut the wrapping paper and pinching the bridge of my nose. "Was there a particular reason you called?"

"Yes," she huffs, sensing my desire to rush her off the call. "I wanted to know when we can expect you back for Christmas."

This is awkward. I thought I made it clear the other times we spoke that I wasn't going to be home for the holidays this year.

"I know you won't make it home for the church toy drive, but I was thinking—"

"I'm not coming home anytime soon. I told you that. I'm working those days."

"Who works on Christmas?! That's a day for people to spend with their families."

"Lots of people work Christmas. Firemen, nurses, concession stand workers at the Timberwolves games, gas station employees—"

"Point made, Mia. But you are none of those things."

"But I am working at a resort where people are spending their Christmas and expecting services. I am hosting most people's holiday events. It's what most of them are paying for."

"I never thought I'd see the day where my only daughter wouldn't come home to see her family. This could be your nonna's last, you know."

Wow. She is laying the guilt on thick. Nonna is healthy as a horse. She may outlive us all.

"If that's all you wanted—" I begin.

"One more thing. When are you going to put poor Steven out of his misery? The man has been a mess since you left. I know we were all riding you hard to get him to commit, but we didn't think you'd take such drastic steps. Mission accomplished. He's ready."

Of course Steven went to my mother about this. He's such a

mama's boy, it bleeds into other families. Unfortunately for him, I'm not letting my family control my fate anymore, and he sure as hell isn't part of my future. I could explain this to her for the twelfth time, but if it hasn't stuck yet, only time will.

I quickly change the subject to my cousin's recent pregnancy announcement and finally get her off the phone after I promise to video call during Christmas breakfast.

Before returning to my wrap job, I shoot off a text to the last number Steven texted me from.

> Stop going to my family. If you want to be a Ricci so bad, Nonna has been single for years. Have at it.

Reblocking him, I turn my attention back to Opal's present. I don't know her well, but I'm hoping a copy of *The Baking Bible* and some adorable oven mitts are to her liking. She probably doesn't need the recipes, but the book will look pretty on a shelf.

As soon as I put the finishing touches on my gift, a knock sounds at my door. Knowing it's Jamie and that he has a universal entry card, I shout for him to come in.

"Well, isn't this a sight," he greets as he swaggers over to me sitting on my heels, cleaning up the mess. "What's that?"

"My Secret Santa gift. Opal was tough to buy for, but I think I nailed it."

"She couldn't have been tougher than Hadley."

A hiss escapes my lips because, yeah. She would be hard to buy for. When I feel his presence behind me, I look over my shoulder and take him in. No matter how many times I see him in his flannel and Henley combo, it is mouthwatering.

"Those are some high-quality wrapping supplies," he comments, picking up the red ribbon I used to add flair to the shiny green paper. "Do you have any more presents to wrap?"

Just his, but I don't want to tell him I got him one yet in case we aren't exchanging gifts. He doesn't strike me as the ribbon detail kind of guy anyway. A mischievous grin spreads across his cheeks when I shake my head.

"So this ribbon is up for grabs?"

"If you want?" I answer hesitantly.

"Stand up," he says, tone stern.

"What?"

"Stand. Up."

Curious to see what he has in mind, I obey. When I'm up, he reaches his hand out to snatch my ponytail and pull me into him, lips fusing with mine. I am so consumed with the kiss, I don't notice that he's gathered my hands in front of me until I feel the velvety side of the ribbon circle them.

"What are you doing?" I question breathily.

Bringing his lips to my ear, he whispers, "Tying you up like the pretty present you are."

At his words, he rips one end of the ribbon off the spool and binds my wrists together. A thrill surges through me as I test the security of the knot.

Leading me by the ribbon, Jamie pulls me toward the sofa where he sits, legs spread. His gaze travels down my pajama-clad body. "This little outfit is killing me, baby. How many of these silky sets do you have?"

"A few," I say, breath hitching as his nimble fingers slowly undo the buttons of my top until it splays open, bearing my chest.

Rubbing his thumb softly over each nipple, he admires my breasts before his hands travel to the hem of my sleep shorts, which he quickly pushes down. "You look so sexy like this, Mia. I'm never going to get over these juicy tits. I want to watch them bounce in my face. What do you say? You want to ride my cock while I play with them?"

Fuck yes, I do. That sounds incredible. The only problem is that I'm nervous. My ex never outright said it, but I got the impression I wasn't very good on top. Immediately sensing my shift in confidence, Jamie asks what's wrong.

"I don't have a lot of experience in this position. What if it isn't good for you?"

"Mia, there is no way any position that has your perfect pussy squeezing my cock won't be amazing, but if you want, I can talk you through it. How does that sound?"

"You'd do that?"

"I don't know if you've noticed, but I find telling you what to do hot as fuck."

I laugh, because I actually have noticed that and I am in complete agreement.

"First, let's make sure you're nice and ready for me." Jamie slides his fingers in between my folds, focusing in on my clit before he teases my entrance.

"You're soaked. Is this all for me?"

"Yes," I moan as he slides two fingers inside me and scissors the way that I love. When his thumb finds my clit, it doesn't take long for me to come apart on his hand. Once I do, he forces me to take a step back and strips off his flannel and undershirt.

"Undo my belt."

With my hands tied, it takes a bit of maneuvering to get his belt and button undone. Once I do, I push them down his legs, where he steps out them. "Boxers, too," he demands huskily.

When his boxers hit the floor, he sits back down on the couch, this time with his legs closer together. "Loop your hands around my neck and straddle my lap."

Doing as he asks, I hook my bound wrists over his head and put my knees on each side of his hips. "I wish I could watch you position me at your entrance, but we'll have to save that for next time," he notes, breath ghosting my neck. "I'm going to help you get it in the right spot, and then I want you to slide down on it, okay? Go at your own pace."

"Okay."

Kissing my lips, he moves the tip of his cock to my entrance and pushes the head in. Moving slowly, I sink down several inches, reveling in the way he fills me. It has felt incredible in every position, but in this one where I control the tempo and angle, it feels even better.

"That's it, baby," he coaxes. "Keep going. I know how much your greedy cunt likes to take all of me." My core clenches at his words and I slide down further. As I do, Jamie's lips return to my neck, where he kisses and sucks bites down one side before the other.

We both groan when I take him to the hilt, and I pause, unsure what to do next. From the porn I've seen, I know I need to bounce up and down on him, but I'm not sure how.

"Use your hands on the back of the couch as leverage," he prompts as if hearing my thoughts. Rising a few inches, I slam back down. I feel so full of him.

"How's that, baby?" he grunts.

"Good. How is it for you?"

"Perfect. But don't worry about me right now. Figure out what you like. The more you enjoy it, the more I'll enjoy it." He places his hands on my hips and swivels them, hitting spots that make me see stars.

I let out an unintelligible noise when he repeats the motion. "That the spot? Hit it yourself, baby. Show me what you can do."

I take his encouragement and ride with it, so to speak. I try different speeds, angles, and patterns, until I find one that makes my legs quake. Between the self-edging and the way Jamie reaches down to flick my clit, I eventually shudder into a hard release.

When I come back to myself, Jamie is running his hands soothingly up and down my back. "You did so good," he coos. When I make a move to get off him, I realize my hands are still tied in place behind his head. Squirming, I also notice his dick is still hard inside me.

"You didn't come?"

"Not yet," he rasps. "I've done a lot of difficult things in my life, but none were as hard as not following you over the edge."

"Why didn't you?" I ask shyly.

"You didn't think I tied you up just for you to have all the fun, did you? I got plans for you, sweet girl. And they mostly include securing you to the headboard and torturing you the way you tortured me."

"I didn't torture you! You're the one who chose not to come."

"That's true," he muses. "I guess I should just keep making you come until I do, then."

In one smooth motion, Jamie stands, walking over to the bed and laying me down. A sense of emptiness fills me when he slides out, but it's quickly replaced with anticipation when he grabs the discarded ribbon and rips off another strand.

"Get comfy, baby. You're in for a long night." And he wasn't kidding.

19

Mia

Last night's activities left me perfectly relaxed, which I needed for the frenzy of a day that greeted me. Even though the staff Christmas party was supposed to be no work for Sugar Peak employees, I still took care of arranging most of it.

Hadley tried to insist she had it under control, but that woman works hard enough. She deserved to enjoy it as well. Plus, I joined the team later than most, so I was happy to organize it.

"Everything looks great," Hadley says when she walks into the library an hour before the party begins. "Rory was right. You were perfect for this role."

My cheeks heat at the compliment and I thank her. "I know your initial contract was only through the end of the season, but how would you feel about making this a more permanent thing?"

"Really?"

"Absolutely. You've done a fantastic job, and if you're willing to stay, we'd love to have you. I don't know how long Mr. Oliveira and I will stay. It would be nice to know we're leaving Sugar Peak in capable hands."

"I would love to!" I exclaim. I'm surprised how much lighter I feel at Hadley's offer. I've been doing my best to live in the moment and not think about what comes next, but a part of me was scared.

"Excellent. Let's chat more after we get past the new year. Also, Mr. Oliveira isn't sure if he's going to make it to the party tonight, so he wanted me to give you your gift now."

"He got me a gift? Wasn't the holiday bonus enough?" The extra money that hit my bank account was much more generous than I expected, having only been here a few weeks.

"He was your Secret Santa," she informs me.

"He participated?" She nods. "Who had him?"

"I did, actually. I got him something really special, but he'll have to wait to get it. Anyway, I'll let you wrap up your last minute prep. I saw Megan helping Vicki bring in the catering, so we should be all set soon."

Moments after Hadley leaves, Megan and her mother come in. Sharing an office, the pair of us have become fast friends. We have a lot in common, both being small town girls.

"That's a big smile," she comments. "Did a grinchy handyman deck your halls before I came in here?"

It takes a moment for her joke to register. "No, better! Hadley offered me a permanent position at the resort."

"That's amazing! I was hoping you'd have a *The Holiday* ending."

"A what?" I laugh.

"You know, how Cameron Diaz and Kate Winslet both

found love and a new life in the cities they were visiting? You did it, too. Great job, hunky handyman..."

"I wouldn't say I 'have' Jamie," I say, mood dampened by that revelation.

"Please," she scoffs, "I may not have known him long, but that man is gone for you. You were both holding back from the unknown, but now you can give it a real shot."

Before I get the chance to respond, her mom calls her over to help, and I'm left at the games table. Is she right? Was I holding myself back from Jamie? It's a paradox. On one hand, I've never been closer to or trusted anyone more than I do him. On the other, there is so much we don't know about each other.

The path I've envisioned for my life has taken a complete one-eighty in the last month. At this point, I don't know what future I want. Did I want my old one simply because it was what was expected? Unfortunately, I don't have time to process all these thoughts. I've got a party to throw.

As four rolls around, my coworkers begin filing in. I try to greet and chat with everyone, but I can't help but find myself waiting for a certain one. It doesn't take long for him to walk in with Spencer and a familiar furry blockhead.

"Crosby." I smile when the canine makes a beeline straight for me. Bending down, I pat his head, accepting his kisses. "Hi, boy! I'm so glad you could make it."

"We couldn't have a party without our unofficial mascot," Spencer asserts when he makes his way over. "Though I am jealous of the greeting he gave you. I'm starting to think I've been replaced as his favorite person."

"I'm his favorite person," Jamie notes dryly.

"Keep telling yourself that, buddy. I've never seen him that excited to see you."

"I can't blame him for wanting attention from the pretty

girl, especially with the way she's working that elf hat. If I'm a good boy, will you sit on my lap later?"

I flush at the innuendo, surprised he's being this brazen in public. He maintains some decorum when he leans forward and whispers for only me to hear. "Maybe we can check number seven off the list tonight and have some fun in the supply closet while our coworkers are none the wiser."

"Maybe," I reply breathlessly. "You're in a good mood."

"Sunny gave him his gift early since she has to work the front desk. It was some special cocktail mix she had made just for him. Said it would 'infuse him with the holiday spirit,'" Spencer explains.

"Is that how you convinced him to wear the *Frozen* sweater?" Spencer shrugs, but I catch the mischief dancing in his expression. I'm going to have to ask what's in that mix.

Taking a step back from the pair, I clear my voice, attempting to not let too much happiness bleed through at my no-longer-so grinchy man. "You two enjoy the party. Oh, and Olaf, I have some news to share with you later."

The statement appears to give Jamie pause as he sizes me up, and not in the sexy way he was earlier. "Can I get a hint?"

"It's something that I've been hoping would happen for a while and now that it has. We need to talk about what it means for the future."

I don't mean to sound cryptic, but there is no good way to talk around it without giving it away. I hope he's going to be happy about the news, but we went into this relationship—if I can even call it that—with the idea that it might have an eventual end date in mind.

As the party goes on, my nerves increase over talking with Jamie, but the festivities distract me. I laugh so hard watching two of the lift operators play the reindeer pantyhose game, I almost fall out of my seat. I can't remember the last time I was this light; had this much fun. Even on my annual friends' trip to Michigan, there was underlying tension wanting to ensure everything went smoothly. The only thing I'm worried about tonight is not letting Brooks get me too drunk with his delicious cocktails.

The gift exchange is also a hoot. I'm pleased to see people took it seriously—some maybe too seriously. Hadley got Spencer new pink-tinted goggles that I am sure are over the spend limit. She joked that since he saw the world through rose-colored glasses, he might as well see the slopes the same way.

Jamie gifted Hadley a travel-themed adult coloring book, picturing many of the places she'd been to with Thiago. Megan found the most beautiful antique hair accessories for Sunny, and she gushed about them profusely to me when I saw her earlier at the desk.

When it's Megan's turn, the atmosphere shifts drastically.

"I'm going to guess a man is my Santa." She laughs, picking up her haphazardly wrapped gift. When she manages to get through the duct tape, she stares at the contents, stunned.

"Is this a joke?" she demands. Anger and hurt lace her tone. I try to get a peek at what's inside, but her hands block my view. Her watery glare is locked on Spencer. His jovial expression is squashed by her reaction. He must have been the one who gifted her.

"Tink—" he starts

"No!" she roars. "This is low, even for you!"

Everyone watches the exchange wide-eyed. Concerned for my friend, I move to comfort her, but when she realizes we're all witnessing the scene, she bolts. Sparing a glance at Spencer, he appears perplexed and embarrassed as he stares at the door she disappeared out of. Clearly, he isn't going to go after her. Not wanting her to be alone, I do.

She wasn't in our office or any of the rooms downstairs. I'm starting to wonder if she went home when I make it to the lobby and scan for her. As I do, my vision stops on a familiar but completely out of place figure. I blink, assuming I must be imagining it: Steven in the Sugar Peak lobby.

"There you are, babe!" he yells as he crosses over to me.

Why is he here? And why is he calling me babe? I'm going to ream whichever one of my family members let it slip that I was here. I should have known when I told my gossipy cousins about the famous figure skaters staying with us that they would have been able to determine where I was. I'm surprised the FBI hasn't scooped them up by now.

"I can see you're speechless." He grins, leaning down to kiss me.

I jolt back, so he is forced to connect only with my cheek. "What are you doing here?"

"I came to get you. Your family is bummed you aren't coming home for the holidays, so I decided it's best to end this charade and bring you back. I'm saving Christmas."

There is a lot to unpack with that statement. I must still be in shock that he's here because no response comes to mind as I continue to stare at him. Taking my silence as encouragement, he gives me what I think is supposed to be a playful eye roll and drops down to one knee.

As he's reaching into his pocket, my brain comes back online and I realize what he's doing, and no. Absolutely not. Before he can get the words out, I'm pulling him up and tugging him to the corner of the cafe. We're already drawing attention from those who thought a proposal was about to take place. I don't need more people gawking at us as I turn him down or, more aptly, talk sense into him.

"What do you think you're doing?!" I whisper-shout to him.

"Proposing! Like you wanted," he huffs, agitated. He's

scowling at me, as if I ruined some magical moment he had planned.

"Why would you do that?"

"You told me to!"

"I did no such thing," I assert.

Steven sighs. "Yes, you did. You told me I had to propose by Christmas—which you didn't make easy, by the way, disappearing to another country."

"I didn't disappear. I left. Trummings, my life, and you. I didn't leave so you'd chase me. I left to start over."

"But now you don't have to. Your tantrum worked. I'm proposing. You can come home. We'll get married in the summer and we can start popping out those babies you want," he replies matter-of-factly. His blasé attitude over these huge life events would be cutting if I cared anymore.

At this point, I don't know if I want to be married. Someday, maybe. But now that I've got a taste of the world outside my small town, I'm eager to explore it. If I get married along the way, fine. But that status symbol isn't the end goal the way it used to be.

"I'm not throwing a tantrum," I silently seethe.

"I don't understand what you want, Mia," he replies, tone turning harsh now that he realizes I'm not planning to fall into his arms at the minimal effort he's put in. "You wanted to get married, so I'm marrying you."

"Don't sound so thrilled about the prospect." I laugh humorlessly. "I didn't want to get married." He eyes me pointedly. Okay, he's got me there.

"I didn't *just* want to get married. I wanted a partner who cares about me, respects me, and genuinely likes me. Three things you haven't shown me you do in a while."

"I like you," he argues. "You're a great cook. Your family is welcoming, and you always make sure I have what I need."

"All of those things are about you!"

"What?"

"None of those things are attributes about me that you like. They're all things I offer you. Any girl with a nice family could be slotted into your life and you probably wouldn't notice. There are plenty of girls like that back home. Can you honestly name one thing specific to me that you love?"

I watch as he thinks for a moment. I can tell some bullshit is about to spew from his mouth, so I cut him off. "We're done, Steven. Even if you had the world to give me, I wouldn't want it. I've outgrown my old life and even though I don't know where this one will take me, for the first time in a long time, I'm excited for what's ahead."

"So you aren't coming back with me?"

"I'm not," I reply.

"What am I supposed to tell your mom?"

"The truth? Nothing? I don't care. If she wants to talk about it, she can contact me. But she knows where I stand."

Rolling my shoulders to release the tension this conversation has placed there, I continue. "I think it's best if you go home. I have to find my friend, and there is nothing here for you. I wish you the best."

With those words, I walk past a stunned Steven and renew my search for Megan, and my new life.

20

JAMIE

THE SPECIAL COCKTAIL mix Sunny gifted me for Secret Santa had me feeling lighter than I had in years. She told me it would cure my "inner Grinch" and she may have been right, because I had a blast at the party. Mostly, anyway.

Mia's pronouncement has been playing at the back of my mind. I have no idea what it could be and I have to say, I'm a bit nervous about it. She may as well have asked if we could "talk" later. The games and present exchange were a great distraction until the vibes went downhill after Megan opened her gift from Spencer. He looked equally upset by her reaction.

I should check in with him about it, but first, I need to talk to Mia. I'm supposed to go up to the townhouse chalets in the morning to make repairs before a guest checks in and I don't want to be stuck wondering what she wanted to say all night.

Opal does her best to bring the mood back up at the party,

but with both Spencer and Mia gone, I have no more reason to stay. Indicating for Crosby to follow, we make our way to the main floor in search of our girl.

Because more and more, that's what she feels like. Ours. Mine. I'm hoping her news is that she wants me to be hers, too. Because God knows I am. I think I have been since the day Crosby knocked her into my arms. Damn, I need to ask Sunny what was in that drink because it's making a sap out of me.

Speaking of Sunny, when I make it to the lobby, she is squaring off at the front desk with a stocky man. I know she can hold her own, but if I can lend some of my tall white man privilege to her interaction, I want to help.

"How can there be no rooms?" I hear him shout as I approach.

"As I've told you, sir. We are fully booked for the holidays. The bed and breakfast further down the mountain has some availability. I recommend you try there or return to the city."

"I don't want to return to the city. I spent all day traveling to this resort and my girlfriend is here."

"Then I suggest you talk to her," Sunny supplies, a hint of mischief in her eyes.

"Everything okay here?" I ask.

"Do you work here?"

"I do," I reply, crossing my arms as I lean a hip against the counter. Crosby sits stiffly beside me, growling lowly. He rarely growls. He must get the same bad vibes I do from this guy. "What seems to be the problem?"

"As I was explaining to the girl, my girlfriend works here. I came to surprise her and propose. I can't do that if I'm not actually here."

Sunny starts to interject, but he keeps going. "I've had a long day of traveling and I want to rest before talking to Mia again."

At Mia's name on his lips, I freeze. My mind spins, not latching on to a single thought as the sound of my blood rushing between my ears grows louder.

"Are you Steven?" I ask

He puffs his chest. "Yeah. My girl has been talking about me? All good things, I hope." None of them were good. But I don't tell him that. Instead the words 'my girl' replay over and over in my head.

"Anyway, as I was telling the receptionist, I came to propose to Mia. She said I had to by Christmas, so here I am. It's time for her to come home."

"Didn't she just—"

I cut Sunny off, wanting to get away from this interaction I've inserted myself into. "As she said, we don't have any room. We book up for Christmas years in advance. You'll have better luck down the mountain or in Vancouver. Shuttle goes back into town every few hours. I'd check with Kevin."

"But my—" I can't hear him call Mia his girlfriend one more time. Turning on my heel, I walk straight out the door. I don't know where I'm going, but I know I need to get out. My mind is reeling.

Is this what Mia wanted to talk about? She wanted to tell me Steven was back and she was leaving? I know we didn't make each other any promises, but I thought we had time. Time to get to know each other. Time to form a connection outside of sex. It's ironic that I wanted to show her how she could have pleasure without strings, but now I'm desperately wishing I tied her to me somehow.

I can't believe she would throw what we have away. Who am I kidding? She put in a decade with that douche. I'd be a fool to think she'd pick me over him. He's embedded into her life in a way I'll never be able to be.

I know I should man up and face her, but I don't have it in

me right now. As I trudge through the snow, I spot Spencer sitting on a bench near the ice skating rink, head in his hands. I really want to be alone right now, but my time at Sugar Peak and with Mia has me valuing my connections with people. As shitty as I feel, he looks just as bad.

"You good?" I ask, sitting next to him. Crosby noses his face between his hands so that he can lick his face.

"Meh," he sighs.

"Want to talk about it?"

"No."

If I was in a less self-pitying mood, I'd be more worried that my typically boisterous friend is giving me monosyllabic answers.

"Want to go up the mountain and hammer some shit?"

That question shifts his gaze from my dog up to me. Searching my expression, he must see I'm serious and he nods accordingly.

⁂

Several hours and half a dozen beers later, Spencer and I have made good work on repairing the leak in the townhouse kitchen. Reinsulating the repaired pipe and patching the ceiling was a good distraction for both of us. Unfortunately, now the only thing left to do is literally watch the paint dry.

"Here," Spencer says, handing me another beer.

"Thanks."

He nods. We sit in silence for a few long moments before he breaks it. "I know why I'm upset and down for demo at 2 a.m., but what's your reason? I'm not complaining by any means, but I figured you'd be with Mia tonight and do this in the morning."

His lips tip slightly when my reply is a grunt. This whole having-real-friends thing is new to me. Not that I haven't had any before, but with how often I moved, I kept most of my relationships surface level. It's easier that way. Now, though, I find myself genuinely wanting to share, but I'm not sure how.

Contemplating what to say, I pick at the edges of the beer label, making a pile of tiny shreds in front of me. "Mia's ex is back," is all I come up with.

"Oh, shit. The one from North Dakota?"

"Yeah. I saw him in the lobby earlier tonight. He said he came to propose."

"Wow. That's some Mike Hannigan shit right there."

"Who?"

"Mike Hannigan." Sensing my confusion, he adds, "Paul Rudd."

Still not sure who he's talking about, I stare at him blankly.

"Have you never seen Friends, man?"

"I've seen episodes here and there."

"Uncultured swine," he mutters. "We can deal with that later. So Mia's engaged to the loser and leaving?"

"Probably."

"Probably? What do you mean probably? What did she say when you talked to her about it? You did talk to her about it, didn't you?"

I shrug, much to his dissatisfaction.

"Bro! You are not living the miscommunication trope right now. That is the worst one."

"Sometimes you speak, and it's like a foreign language," I grouse, because what the fuck is the miscommunication trope?

"We'll deal with your lack of pop culture later. For now, you need to talk to Mia."

"What's to talk about? They were together for ten years. Her family loves him. He's her brother's friend. He's in. I'm out. I was just the rebound to get some experience with while she waited on her ex to get his shit together."

He winces at my description, but shakes it off quickly. "I don't think Mia would play you or anyone like that. From what I could tell, she had genuine feelings for you."

"I don't think she played me, either. At least not on purpose. It'd be easier, though. How can I compete with a proposal? I mean, I like her. A lot. I may even love her, but it's been a month. I can't offer her forever like he can."

"Are you sure that's what she wants? To be married? Forever? From the time I've spent with her, she seems to be enjoying her time out of her small town. She may have been ready to settle down there, but from what I can tell she isn't ready to be rooted down so soon."

Hope blooms in my chest. Is he right? Mia seemed very over her ex every time we talked about him. I can't imagine she's dying to go back to the guy who hardly made her come and never ate her out. Not sure how she could give that up having seen—and felt—how much she enjoys that first hand… and mouth.

I meant it when I said I may love Mia. She's the kind of woman I can see forever with. She's sweet and funny. Her tenacious mission to get me to love Christmas, for the simple fact it would give me joy, was endearing as hell. I think we could really have something if we gave it a chance. But is that enough?

I don't want her to pick me over Steven. I mean, I do. But I don't want to worry that I held her back from a stable life surrounded by family. I want her to choose herself, and let me be a sidekick along the way.

"I can see your wheels spinning," he comments casually, a smug grin stretched across his smug face.

"Yeah, yeah. We did me. Now what's got your goat?" I ask.

"Let's just say not all brothers are as cool about their friends dating their sisters as Mia's is. And caring about that cost me the girl I always wanted."

I want to push more on what he means or if that girl is Megan, but I can tell he isn't ready to go there.

Standing, I dump the remainder of my beer in the sink. I need Mia to know she has other options aside from Steven and home. That she can build a future here. But first, I need to sober up. Neither Spencer nor I are sober enough to take the ATVs back down to the lodge.

"That's the spirit!" he replies. "Let's plan your grand gesture."

"Grand gesture?"

"I have so much to teach you. Planning first, explaining later."

21

ONCE I FOUND MEGAN, she was halfway into a bottle of wine. Joining her, it turned into two bottles and staying up half the night, laughing at Steven's audacity and lamenting the stupidity of men. She finally let me in on the mystery that surrounded her and Spencer, and I made a silent vow to help the pair work through their issues.

That problem is for another day, though. Today I am fighting for my life hosting a Christmas Eve Mahjong tournament with a hangover. My shitty feeling was exacerbated by running into Steven at breakfast this morning. It took another long talk and going into explicit detail about all the ways he failed me as a partner for him to get the hint and leave. I think he did it more for his ego than anything. As long as it made him go home, I don't care what the reason was.

The tournament is blessedly chill and quiet. While good

for my headache, it's not good for my headspace. I texted Jamie both last night and this morning, but haven't heard anything back. I'm trying not to freak out and assume that he knows my news and is avoiding me because he doesn't want something more permanent, but the hangxiety is alive and well.

I mentioned my Christmas Eve tradition of enjoying the Feast of the Seven Fishes with my family. When I was a kid, my cousins and I would huddle together and watch *Home Alone* before falling asleep at our respective houses. Then on Christmas Day, we'd meet back up and watch the sequel while comparing our presents from Santa.

I had hoped Jamie would join me for an anchovy pizza and *Home Alone* marathon—one through three only, the rest are garbage—but it seems I may be the one left alone tonight. I don't blame him. I am feeling particularly emotional about all this. It's probably a lot to ask your situationship to spend a major holiday with you while you're sad to be away from your family.

I didn't realize how hard that would be until this morning when the reality of it hit me. This is the first Christmas since I've been alive that I won't be with my family. I won't secretly funnel my scallops onto Tony's plate in exchange for his calamari. I won't hear my cousin Dina and her boyfriend-turned-husband fighting over whatever drama is following them this year.

It doesn't help that I've been avoiding my mother's calls. She is not very happy to learn I turned down Steven's proposal. To her, there is no greater achievement than settling down, but I've 'settled' my entire life. I want to try something more. I know that it will be hard for her to wrap her mind around, so it's best to take some space until I have the capacity to explain.

As the games are in full swing, I sneak out my phone to check my texts.

Leave it to Rory to kill it with a Home Alone reference just when I need it.

She tries to send me a picture, but the energy doesn't come through the way she hoped it would. A pang of sadness hits as I see my nonna in the background, holding court with my cousins. Deep down, I know I'm where I need to be, but it sucks at this precise moment.

As the tournament finishes up, I am exhausted and low-level anxious. I would kill for a cuddle and some carbs. Once I have the room cleaned up, I sink into my favorite chair in the library, the one Jamie found me in the night we played in the snow.

As I will myself to return to my room, something wet hits my cheek. Eyes flying open, I am surprised to see Crosby wagging in front of me.

"Hey, buddy," I greet with pats. "Where's your dad?" I scan the room, but don't see Jamie anywhere. Standing, I'm nudged forward by my furry friend. Curious to see what he wants, I let him direct me.

Once he's led me down the hall to the theater room, he nudges the door open and walks inside.

"What are you do—" The words die on my tongue as I take in the room. What was once a movie theater-esque space has been transformed. Making my way to the front, I spin, cataloging all the changes. On one side is a table topped with plate covers and candles.

To the right of that is a fresh-cut Christmas tree. The decorations don't match the others in the hotel. It has a more casual, homey vibe with homemade popcorn garland and tinsel. The opening credits to *Home Alone* are cued up on the screen, and a nest of pillows and blankets litter the front sofa.

Absorbed in checking out the room, I don't notice when Jamie slips out from behind the tree.

"Hi," he says tentatively.

"What is all this?" I ask, cheeks hurting from smiling so hard. Something about my response softens what I'm not realizing is a tense demeanor.

"It's Christmas. For you. But before I give you the details, I have something I want to say."

"Go on." I nod.

Taking in a deep breath, Jamie squares his shoulders. "Don't marry him."

"What?"

"Your douchewad of an ex. Don't marry him. If not for me, for yourself. You deserve so much more than he can offer you."

It suddenly dawns on me that Jamie must've run into Steven at some point. Did he tell him he was proposing? Is that why he's been ignoring me all day? I can't imagine what must've gone through his head. Did he think I would even consider getting back together with Steven after everything I've been through, after everything I've done with him?

A part of me wants to be offended that he thinks I'd go back to Steven, but I get it. It's barely been a month since I left. You'd think that wouldn't be long enough to get over someone, but I think I was getting over Steven a little bit every day for the last several years.

Sensing his nerves, I decide to put Jamie out of his misery.

"I said 'no.'"

"You did?" he asks hopefully.

"I did. That isn't the life I want anymore. I want—I need more than what Steven and Trummings have to offer."

"Thank God," he mutters before pulling me into his arms and taking my mouth in a searing kiss. "I had a whole speech planned to convince you otherwise."

"You can still give it to me," I tease.

He laughs. "The gist of it was that even though I can't give you what he can, the picket fence, Sunday dinners with your family, etc., I care about you and think you—we—deserve a chance to see where this could go. I can't offer you a ring right now—"

"I don't want one," I assert.

He stares down at me with a slightly shocked expression that I want to kiss off his handsome face.

"One day, I will. But I've spent ten years aiming toward that goal and it felt hollow. I want to focus my energy on living my life instead of planning ahead for it. I want to see things and do things and explore who I am in this world. If marriage happens along that journey, great. But it's not the end goal that it used to be."

"I think I might love you," he blurts out, but there is no remorse on his face.

"I think I might love you, too."

Standing on my tiptoes, I cut the distance between us and fuse my lips to his. The kiss isn't as frantic as the first or as many of ours have been in the past—it's filled with promises and potential.

Stepping back, he offers me one of his breathtaking grins. When I move into him again, he stops me. "There will be time for that later. For now, we have dinner to eat, and a movie to watch."

He pulls out a chair and I slide in. "What do we have here?" I ask.

He lifts the plate covers off, and I can't help but fold over in laughter. The combination of foods is crazy. The star of the meal is the delicious smelling Moqueca from the resort's Brazilian steakhouse. But my attention quickly shifts to some of the other items: lobster tail, anchovy pizza, fish and chips, crab cakes, and Goldfish crackers.

"What is all this?" The combination of things is so random, I don't see the obvious theme.

"The Feast of Seven Fishes," he replies sheepishly. "I know it's not what you'd have back home, but it's as close as I could get on short notice. You don't want to know what I had to promise Chef to get some of these items."

My eyes wet with tears at the thoughtfulness of this man. Even while worried I may be considering life with someone else, he was fighting to show me the alternative I could have with him. One filled with kind gestures and... I think those are Swedish fish.

"Thank you," I whisper.

"You're welcome." The expression he gives me is filled with the love growing between us and happiness.

"Okay," he says, clapping his hands and grabbing the remote. "I've been told I need to suspend my knowledge of injuries in order to be convinced these men are only mildly hurt and not dead by this kid's tricks. Shall we dive in?"

And we do. Into the movie. Into the food. And into a future full of unknowns, but that may be what's so exciting about it.

137

22

JAMIE

TAKING the lift back down the mountain, I am impressed and proud of the event Mia put together. X-Games-style ski and snowboarding competitions at the top of the mountain complemented by a crafts fair at the bottom, it is the perfect winter festival.

After our Christmas Eve meal, Mia and I went back to my cabin, where we watched the second *Home Alone* and had a repeat of our holiday ribbon experience, this time with the extra Christmas lights I used to decorate the theater room tree. When we eventually left my bed on Christmas Day for the holiday dinner, Spencer helped me lug the tree home so we could enjoy the festive space.

Mia deemed my holiday bucket list and transformation from Grinch to Who complete. That reminded me that there was still one more item on her list that I could complete from the resort. And watching her now help a little girl at the taffy making station, I see the perfect opportunity to make good on that idea.

"What in the *Nightmare Before Christmas* is going on here?" I laugh as I approach her.

Peering up at me through those pretty brown eyes that sucked me in all those weeks ago, she sighs. "Making taffy from maple syrup was not as easy or mess-free as I expected."

"I can see that. Come on, let's take a break and see if we can get you cleaned up."

Grabbing her hand, I lead her through the resort and into the laundry room. It's the perfect place to check off item number seven: "Up on the Housetop." After filling the sink with soapy water, I carefully pull the sticky plaid shirt over her head. She shivers in just her bra, skirt, and tights.

"Let's warm you up, babe," I coo. Picking her up, I set her down on top of a running dryer. I do this partially for warmth and partially because it puts her exactly at the height I want her to be.

"What are you up to?" she asks playfully.

"You'll see." Reaching into my coat pocket, I pull out the maple candy I made earlier. She eyes it wearily but doesn't comment further.

"You know what I think is so interesting about this candy? You made it by pouring syrup on something cold. In this case, snow. But can you reverse the effects? If I press it against your warm skin, will it melt back down?"

"I-I don't know," she stammers as I bring the candy to her neck. I drop my head to capture her lips in a searing kiss while I move the candy down the side of her neck, over her collar bones and between the breasts I can't get enough of.

When we're both breathless, I lean back and look at the trail of sticky liquid that coats her skin. "My baby is all messy again. Should I clean her up?"

"Yes," she whispers huskily, trying to get off the machine. Stopping her, she gives me a confused expression before understanding dawns on her. "You want to do this here? My room is a few minutes away."

"If we go back to your room, we won't be leaving until I wring every ounce of pleasure out of your perfect body. Besides, I thought you wanted the thrill of almost getting caught. No one is here... right now. If we make it quick, no one will know that I had you screaming in the laundry room while the event went on outside."

"Something tells me this isn't going to be that quick," she replies, head tilting toward the candy in my hand.

"Quick*er*," I drawl. Without allowing her to voice any more reservations, I trace my tongue down the trail of maple syrup. When I get to her tits, I reach behind her to remove the flimsy lace she calls a bra. Even in my lust-addled haze, I'm not dumb enough to ruin something that delicate.

Taking the candy, I circle it around her tight, pink nipple before enclosing my mouth around it. "You taste delicious," I murmur against her. Once I'm confident I've gotten all the syrup, I give her other the same treatment.

The combination of my tongue and vibrations from my voice have her arching her chest into my mouth. Pleased with her reaction, I bring my hand between her parted legs and press the seam of the tights until it is between her lips.

Chest out and hips grinding into my hand, she's never been more beautiful. The need in her eyes is so wanton, it has me ready to give in. "You want me, Mia?"

"Yes," she cries. "Please. No more teasing."

"If you insist." Discarding the candy, I flip up her skirt and use both hands to rip a hole in her tights. She squeals at the action, but her eyes dilate until there is almost no brown to be seen. It seems my girl may enjoy a little primal. Maybe once we finish this list, I can convince her to add that to a new one.

Smiling to myself at the thought, I don't notice that she has undone the button of my jeans until I feel her hand circle my shaft.

"Shit!" I call out as her thumb circles the tip. I allow her a few more strokes before I pull away. "No more of that. I want to finish inside you. Not my own pants."

She pouts dramatically, then parts her legs further. "Then do it," she taunts.

"Careful, baby. This is already going to be quick and dirty. Don't rile me up even more or you won't be able to walk out of here without a limp." Lining up with her center, she's already pushed her panties to the side, giving me full access to her glistening cunt. I tap her clit with my tip a few times before I shift down to her entrance.

In one hard thrust, I am inside her. Her back bows at the intrusion, and she calls out my name. Her hands, which were resting on the edge of the dryer, grip my shoulders for purchase as I begin to push in and out of her.

"You feel so good," I coo. "You were made for this. Made to be pleasured. Made for me."

Indecipherable words come out of her mouth as her nails dig into me. It's hard enough that I know she'll leave crescents behind, and I revel in wearing her marks.

Knowing she needs more to push her over the edge I'm so quickly approaching, I pull her ass forward until she's almost hanging off. In this new position, I can tilt her hips, allowing me to hit the spot I know makes her see stars.

"Jamie. Jamie. Jamie," she chants.

"I know, Mia. I got you. Just a little bit more. I need you to come for me. Can you do that, baby? Can you clamp this pussy around my cock and shatter for me?"

As if the words were all she needed, she breaks apart beautifully in my arms. Three thrusts later, I follow behind.

Stilling inside her, I lean my head against her shoulder and catch my breath.

"That was..." she pants.

"Yeah," I agree.

I give her a quick kiss before begrudgingly pulling out from her sweet heat. Rebuttoning my fly, I hand her back her bra and watch her look around quizzically. "Uh, Jamie? Where is my top?"

Fuck. I didn't think about that. Her shirt is still soaking in the sink. Her confusion turns to humor when she realizes the same thing.

"Off!" she demands, motioning at my torso.

"You want my shirt?"

"Well, I need something to wear, and seeing as you always have on a flannel *and* a Henley, you have one to spare."

"Fine," I concede. "But later, I want you spread across the bed in nothing but this shirt so I can get a real taste of you. Every inch."

"Deal."

Handing Mia the shirt. I watch as she twists and tucks the oversized flannel in a way that makes her outfit seem planned and effortless. Not a moment too soon because when we open the door to leave, Spencer is standing on the other side.

"There you are. Can you help with the skating rink lights? A few of them—" He stops mid sentence when he sees the pretty blush that colors Mia's cheeks. "Well, well well. What do we have here?"

I send him a glare for embarrassing her, but there is no heat behind it. I know he means no harm. "Come on, let's go see about some lights, and then maybe I can show off the skating skills that got me banned from the Whistler Community Rink."

Hours later, sitting at the fire pit sounded by our friends, I'm struck by the thought that the holidays aren't that bad after all.

Epilogue

JAMIE

"Do we have to go back?" Mia whines from the hammock beside me. We've spent the last thirteen days ziplining and drinking Pina Coladas in Costa Rica.

A year after she got it, Mia finally cashed in on the Secret Santa gift Thiago gave her—a two-week stay at one of his other resorts. We considered going last year after the season ended, but decided to drive around the northern US instead since neither of us had traveled much.

We drove from Seattle all the way to her hometown to spend a tense Fourth of July with her family. Her mom wasn't thrilled to see her daughter living a different life than she'd planned, but I won her father and brother over. I count it as a win.

After road tripping through Minneapolis, Chicago, and

Cleveland, we ended our trip at Niagara Falls and headed back into Canada. This year, we decided to take it easy and relax on the beach, with a few adventures to keep it interesting. Tomorrow, we head back to Sugar Peak to start preparations for the ski season.

After two successful seasons, we've got this in the bag. But it's always nice to go home. Mia officially moved into my cabin last year and we've done our best to make it a home. I even let her go all out with Christmas decorations.

"Unfortunately, we do," I reply, pulling her closer.

"But the monkeys will miss us," she pouts.

"I think they'll be happy to move on to whatever tourist feeds them next."

Sighing, she nuzzles back down into me, and we nap in the Costa Rican heat.

Later that night while Mia's in the shower, I notice a piece of paper on her nightstand. I can't help but chuckle when I realize it's her original naughty list. Everything is checked off except *Holiday in the Sun*. Seeing that I've made love to her no less than three times out on our private beach during this trip, I think it's safe to mark it off.

When I go to do so, I notice for the first time that there is something written on the back. In bold letters at the top, it reads *Mia's Naughtier List*. The first item is already marked through. Tilting it under the light, I see it reads, *The Polar Express* (chased down and fucked).

As if I summoned her, I peek up to find Mia not in the shower as I thought, but staring back at me, list in hand. Before I can speak, she beats me to it as she turns to run out the patio door.

"Catch me if you can!"

Want to meet Mia and Steven before the break? They have a big cameo in *Zealous Intentions*, a fake dating romance with a badass publicist and sexy tattoo artist.

Sugar Peak Sneak Peak

A Naughty List for Christmas is the first book in the Sugar Peak Resort series. Get more of your favorite characters by checking out the rest of the series!

Brooks and Hadley's story is up next in, *My Ex for Christmas*! Below is an excerpt from that story.

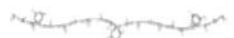

Hadley

"Why didn't you tell me you were coming home, bitch?"

I sigh as I step back into my suite after another long day. With my phone in one hand and my bag in the other, I have to kick the door closed with my foot. "I was a little preoccupied getting everything sorted for Mr. Oliveira's takeover of the ski resort."

On the other end of the line, my sister makes a noise of

protest. "After all these years, he still makes you call him *Mr. Oliveira?*"

"No," I reply, a little defensively. In fact, my boss often tells me *not* to call him Mr. Oliveira. He prefers Thiago. "I just like keeping things professional."

I can practically feel her eye roll through the phone. "Hadley."

"Samantha."

"Please tell me you haven't been pulling twelve-hour days."

"I haven't been pulling twelve-hour days."

They're usually sixteen. But at least I take a break for lunch. That has to count for something, right?

She scoffs. "You're at a beautiful resort in the mountains!" Sam says, which she only knows because I was forced to send her pictures this morning. "At least promise me you'll do more than rot in your hotel room every night."

"I do not *rot*," I say with a scoff.

She ignores me. "Do something fun! Go out, have a drink. For me. Please?"

I haven't *gone out* in a long time. Probably not since university. Even then, my wild nights were few and far between. I much preferred staying in to study, and sometimes on the weekends I would venture out to immerse myself in the Brazilian culture. I hadn't wanted to take a minute of my studying abroad for granted.

But I know that if I don't throw my sister a bone, she's going to keep pestering me. She might even resort to driving up here from her new place in Nanaimo and physically dragging me outside to have her definition of fun.

"Ugh. *Fine*, I'll go."

"You better not be lying! I'll know if you are."

Unfortunately, she's right. She has always had this uncanny

ability to sniff out my lies and pry the truth from me. In some ways, she makes a better older sister than I do.

I sigh as I set my bag down on the love seat in my living room. My suite is essentially a small apartment. "I'm going, I'm going."

One drink, I promise myself. I'll go for one drink. Then I can successfully say I followed Sam's orders, and I'll never have to do it again.

"And while you're at it, maybe you can get yourself laid or something."

"Sam!" I chastise. My cheeks flare at the insinuation—that I haven't had sex in a while—and I ignore the fact that she's right.

I can just imagine her satisfied grin. "Okay, I've gotta go, but you have a blast! And don't think this conversation is over. I still want to know why you *really* didn't tell me you were moving back."

"I love you the most," I say.

"I love you the mostest," she replies. "Bye."

I hang up the phone and glance down at my clothing. A wool sweater, black slacks and knee-high suede boots. That will have to do. Not exactly *going out* attire, but I'd rather not waste another outfit. The less time I have to spend worrying about laundry, the more time I have to keep on top of things for Thiago.

Pulling out my phone, I search for the nearest bar. Something tells me Sam wouldn't appreciate me getting my drink from the resort. There appears to be one singular bar in Sugar Peak, which is about half an hour down the mountain. Fitting for such a small town.

I bundle myself up in my coat, toque and mittens, and then I venture through the resort. The lobby is all floor-to-ceiling windows and dark wood, with a stone fireplace as a focal point. Thiago certainly spared no expense.

Once I'm out the front door, the chill wind hits me instantly. Though I haven't used it much since I've stayed bundled up inside the resort, I am thankful my rental car came with heated seats. Living in São Paulo for so long, I became accustomed to the climate; I've forgotten what it's like to live with snow. But I can already recall not being a fan.

I drive the distance into town, white-knuckling the steering wheel the entire way. I never used to bat an eye when driving in the snow, but eight years can make you forget a lot of things.

After a tense thirty minutes, I roll to a stop in a snow-covered parking lot. From the outside, the building is unassuming. There are letters hanging above the door that spell out *Dirty Dick's*, but the S at the end is upside down, half falling off. No one has bothered to fix it, it seems.

I've been staying at the resort for a couple months now, and I've ventured into town a handful of times. I haven't set foot on this end of the main street, though. If Sugar Peak has a wrong side of town, this is it.

My nose wrinkles as I push open the front door of Dirty Dick's. The name is very apt, given the layer of grime that coats everything. But it appears that none of the patrons care. Some kind of lively music plays from a jukebox in the corner, and merry shouts echo across the room from a group gathered around a pool table.

I make a beeline toward the bar, feeling incredibly out of place here. *One drink*, I remind myself. Settling onto the very last stool at the edge of the counter, I try to ignore the sticky surface in front of me.

I slip my coat off my shoulders and drape it across the stool next to me. With any luck, people will assume the seat is taken and avoid trying to sit there. It's been a long day, so I'm not in the mood for idle chitchat.

The bartender makes her way over to me. Her dark hair,

peppered with streaks of grey, is short, the sides shaved close to her scalp. From beneath the sleeves of her black t-shirt, colourful floral tattoos bloom, trailing down her arms.

"What can I get you?" she asks.

My eyes dart around, looking for some kind of menu, but I come up empty. I suppose the locals just *know* what kind of drinks are served here, like some kind of intrinsic knowledge they gain when they turn legal drinking age. Maybe even before. This certainly looks like a place that doesn't check IDs.

"Um," I say, chewing on my lower lip. I take a stab in the dark. "I'll have a gin fizz, please."

The woman starts laughing before I've even finished my sentence. "Honey, do you know where you are? That fancy ass resort is up the mountain," she says, pointing out the window. I just blink, and she shakes her head. "The best I can do is a vodka cran. That, or beer."

A little embarrassed, I attempt to save face. "I'll have whatever you recommend. Surprise me."

With a small smirk, the bartender turns and grabs a tall glass. From one of the taps, she pours a dark liquid. A layer of foam settles across the top once it's full, and some of it spills over the edge and down the side.

She sets it on the counter in front of me. With a wink, she says, "Enjoy."

The first sip I take makes me want to gag. The bartender is watching, though, so I force myself to swallow the bitter liquid. *Fun*, I think to myself. I'm showing Sam that I still know how to have fun—which I *do*.

The second sip goes down easier, but I fear I may never get the horrid taste out of my mouth. A beer connoisseur, I am not.

When the bartender's attention shifts to another customer down the line, my shoulders drop in relief. I'll just pretend to nurse the drink for a while, then I can pay my tab and leave.

Swivelling on my stool, glass in hand, I watch the locals in their natural habitat. The people I've met in Sugar Peak thus far have been nothing short of kind. And although I'm loath to admit it, it *is* nice to be back in Canada. Travelling the world with Thiago has been incredible, but nothing beats my home province. British Columbia is breathtaking, especially up here in the mountains. Even if it is really fucking cold.

When I told my boss about the abandoned ski resort an hour or so away from my hometown, I never thought he would decide to buy the place and have it fixed up. But he did, and now I'm here.

The front door opens, and a group of people come flooding in, a blast of chill winter air with it. Based on their uniforms, they're employees from the resort. The volume instantly increases as they greet others around the room.

I turn back to face the bar, still nursing my disgusting beer. I can feel the bartender watching again, so I raise the glass to my lips to take another swig. At the same time, someone bumps roughly into my back, and cold liquid slides down my chin to my chest, staining the white fabric of my wool sweater.

I hear a vague *sorry* as the person brushes past. But sorry doesn't cover my dry cleaning bill. Or mend my wounded pride.

I grab a tiny square napkin off the bar top—it's a miracle they even have those here—and dab fruitlessly at the front of my sweater. It's no use, though. The ugly splotch has spread, the liquid seeping through to my skin.

Thanks a lot, Sam. This is your fault.

"Here're those glasses you asked for, Luce."

My hand freezes on my chest. I hardly notice the feel of my soggy sweater anymore because *that voice*. I know that voice. But I'm definitely hearing things. I have to be. Otherwise, that means—

“Thanks, Brooksy. Just throw them over there.”

Oh, no. No, no, no.

A small squeak slips from my mouth unbidden. Chin tipped down, I stare at the surface of the bar, hand on my forehead to shield my face from view. Maybe if I sit here long enough without moving, he won’t notice me.

Please don't let him notice me.

I hear footsteps across the floor behind the bar as he sets the box down where Luce instructed. Then, just when I think I might be in the clear, I can sense someone approach. The looming figure seems too big to be Luce, my beer deliverer, but I metaphorically cross my fingers anyway.

“Hi, Hadley,” he says from above me.

I lift my head, resigned, and meet the familiar brown eyes of my ex boyfriend.

“Hi, Brooks.”

Acknowledgments

Novellas are hard. This one was extra hard. I want to send a special shout out to my fellow Sugar Peak writers for building this world with me and keeping me from going crazy in the process.

Thank you to all the readers who showed support for this novella, especially by ARC readers. Y'all keep us going!

About the Author

Kat Summers is a millennial spicy, contemporary romance author living in Tennessee. Her books are filled with just enough angst to hurt your feelings, witty banter to make you laugh, and steamy, swoon-worthy men to make you blush. She creates stories with strong, sassy heroines who can hold their own but love being called a "good girl."

When she isn't writing, she can be found reading (duh) and spending time with her family and furbaby or gossiping over Mexican food. Fueled by Diet Dr Pepper and a dream, Kat is excited to bring the couples that live in her mind to the rest of the world. Follow her for sneak peeks of future projects.

Find her at @katsummerswrites on all the things.

Also by Kat Summers

Nashville Songbirds Series

Behind in the Count

Stepping Up to the Plate

Scoring Position

Backcheck Heart

Broken Chords